# IN THE NICK OF TIME

J. Lee Graham

COVER ART DESIGN by Ken Hornbeck

For Ken

# Chapter One

"Help!"

The covers flew off his body and hit the night table and toppled over the bedside lamp. With a force like a slingshot, Andy Mackpeace scrambled to the edge of the bed and threw up his supper. Spaghetti and potato salad and garlic bread splattered on the floor in large, indigestible chunks.

The sound of footsteps ran down the hallway. His father opened the door and rushed to Andy's bed but stopped short just in time to avoid stepping into the puke. The room reeked of vomit, and Andy was drenched in sweat. He leaned over the bed again with loud wretches of gut wrenching contractions, waiting for anything else to come up. But they were only dry heaves that left him weak. He found it hard to figure out where he was.

"Andy, are you okay?"

"I threw up," he croaked.

"Hang on," his dad said, "the worst is over. I'll be right back."

"It's happening again," Andy swore to himself when his father ran to the bathroom. "It's not going away! It's going to be with me for the rest of my freaking life!"

His father returned. He threw an old dry towel over the mess on the floor and with a wet, warm washcloth, sat down on the bed and wiped his son's face and arms.

"You're having one of those episodes again, right?"

Andy took the washcloth and wiped down his chest

and stomach.

"Here," Mr. Mackpeace said handing him another washcloth, "put this one on your forehead."

It was freezing cold, and Andy's nerves relaxed with relief.

"Do you want to talk about it?"

Andy revisited the thoughts he had when he went to sleep; the checklist of things to do (the Science test for Monday) and things to look forward to (turning thirteen in two weeks), followed by the descent into a dream that was so deceptive-

Andy got nauseous again. He felt stupid for feeling so scared, so he closed his eyes and leaned back onto his pillows. "No, Dad. I'm good. I just don't want to think about it. It makes me sick when I do."

"Andy, what's going on with you?" his father asked, a slight edge in his voice.

This was the fifth nightmare in three months, and they had started in the spring. His father collected the washcloths and returned to the bathroom. Andy heard his mother talking from his parents' bedroom. "He's shaken up," he heard his father answer. "Yeah, he threw up again, same as last time." His mother said something muffled. "Nah, I got it, go on back to sleep, I'll be there in a little while." Mr. Mackpeace came back with more wet towels and cleaned up the vomit, wiped away the smells.

"What time is it?" Andy asked.

"It's 2:30," his dad said.

It was the same every time.

When it happened on a school night, it was even

harder for Andy to get up in the morning, he was groggier than normal. Luckily for Andy, this was a Friday night.

His father checked in one last time. "What else can I do to help? Do you want me to stay? Hang out until you fall asleep?"

"I'm okay now, Dad. Thanks, I feel a lot better. I think I'll wait and talk to Grandma Geri in the morning."

Grandma Geri. Mr. Mackpeace winced.

"That's fine," he said and leaned over and gave Andy a hug. A quiet, "good night," and Mr. Mackpeace glided out the door, shutting it behind him.

As Andy drifted back to sleep, he heard his father say in the other bedroom, "My mother is probably the last person he should talk to!"

# Chapter Two

"I had that dream again last night, Grandma." It was the next morning. Andy was in Grandma Geri's living room where she was folding towels and sorting out laundry. "It wasn't a dark shape, though, like before, they were men, two men."

"Where was it this time: in a school? The woods?"

"A beautiful, big house. It was sunny out and warm and I was alone. I knew that I had taken a wrong turn. If only I hadn't gone in that house, I would have been safe. So when they attacked me, I start running, just like with the other dreams. I had to get out of there!"

"So, could you ever just stop running?" Grandma Geri asked.

Andy shuddered. "You mean, stop running and let them grab me? Grandma, I can't!"

Grandma Geri's face softened. "You're very sensitive, Andy, and that's a powerful gift. But you have to overcome your fears yourself. No magic wand in the world can take care of that. When you can turn around and face it, them, whoever, I guarantee you, it will leave you alone."

"I wish I could."

"Someday you will," she said as she stacked a batch of pillowcases on a shelf. "Someday, you're going to get sick and tired of running, and you'll get so angry you'll turn around and tell it to stop."

Grandmother Geri was Andy Mackpeace's only grandmother. Often, Andy and his grandmother sat outside together, and she taught her only grandson about her special talent.

She communicated with the dead.

"Not the dead, Andy!" Grandma Geri would have poked him in the ribs if she had heard him.

"We never say that word in our profession," she said. "They are 'the ones who have crossed over.' They're on the other side now, and I help people talk to them. Maybe someone here never got a chance to say 'I love you' or has a lot of guilt about something. So, I contact them and help with the conversation. It's really very simple."

Andy's father, when she talked like that, just shook his head or went into the house. "Mom, you're scaring him."

"But I'm not scared, Dad!" Andy would say.

It was true. Around Grandma Geri, Andy wasn't scared. Everywhere else, however, Andy Mackpeace was the kid who was afraid of everything. Andy was nervous about school, getting yelled at, and people.

Report cards were tense moments too. "Could be better," his father said every time a "B" popped up on the paper. So, he got good grades because he was smart, but mostly he got good grades out of fear. Fear of failing, fear of disappointing somebody, fear of disappointing his father.

At night, in bed, Andy reviewed every word, every conversation he had at school and at home hoping his words hadn't made anyone hate him or be mad at him.

Andy Mackpeace was starting his teenage years with a very sour stomach.

# CHAPTER THREE

"It's a dream catcher," said Andy holding up the Native American artifact from out of a birthday gift box. It was a netted ring with feathers and shells hanging from it. Andy's thirteenth birthday was two weeks after his latest scare, and he looked at his newest gift with a sense of relief. "This should do it!"

He and his parents and Grandma Geri were sitting outside on the patio, at the wooden table, for his birthday breakfast. It was warm enough, finally, to be out in the New Hampshire sun; spring was in full sprint heading toward a short, but adventure-filled summer.

"Yes!" said Grandma Geri. She was finishing the rest of a home-baked muffin ("Who bakes? I got these at the organic bakery.") She wore a wide skirt, full of rainbow colors. In her hair was a headband of golden snakes, like something Cleopatra would have worn. "This particular dream catcher was made by an Ojibwa Shaman," she said to Mrs. Mackpeace. "A woman. She gave it to me when I was in Saskatchewan."

With the legacy Andy's grandfather gave her after he had died, Grandma Geri traveled in the winter all over the world and, like some rare, exotic bird, returned every spring to her home, to Andy and his family, in Silver Lake, New Hampshire. Her ritual was always the same when she stepped out of her car. She greeted Andy with a smile, took his face in her right hand and kissed his left cheek. She could outrun her own sons, she could out dance everyone at any family wedding, and she had one of the gentlest spirits Andy Makepeace would ever know.

"What does it do?" asked Andy's mom.

"It's a healing element," Andy said. "It helps people sleep peacefully at night."

"Absolutely," his grandmother smiled. "According to the Ojibwa, a dream catcher filters a person's dreams. Bad dreams stay in the net, disappearing with the light of day."

"Oh for the love of Pete," Andy's dad said, rolling his eyes toward his mother. "Mom! What possessed you to get that?"

"Now your brother James has one," Geri started to explain. "And ... ."

"Well, then no wonder!" retorted her son, laughing while buttering some more toast. "I'm sure it's hanging right next to his mirror!"

Andy's Uncle James lived in Boston. Unlike Andy or his father, James had dark hair. He was ruggedly built and had a funny tendency to look endlessly at himself in the mirror. It was the running joke anytime he got together with Andy's family, and he sheepishly admitted his own vanity.

"How often do you look in the mirror, Uncle James," Andy once asked.

"Every chance I get."

Uncle James was seven years younger than Andy's father and was much more carefree about life than his stuffy, university professor brother. He was a single man who worked as a Boston tour guide and was going to graduate school part time. Andy liked talking with him. Sometimes he could tell him things he couldn't tell his father.

Andy surveyed his gifts, his family, and took a deep breath of satisfaction on this sunny day. His uncle had sent him a fly rod fishing pole, his parents had given passes to Six Flags for him and his friend Roger, and next to the passes was a book entitled THE UNIVERSE, a 340 page book full of color photos of planets, star clusters, nebulae, galaxies, and quasars. It was astonishing.

He saved Grandma Geri's birthday card to open for last. He did this every year. This time, the card was a photograph of a constellation, shot on a crystal clear night. "It's Gemini!" he said, showing the photo to the group. "It's my Zodiac sign." He opened the card. In Grandma Geri's perfect penmanship, she had written:

*Dear Andy,*
*May you forever discover the wonders of this world, but more importantly, the unfolding of your dreams.*
*Happy Birthday, you sweet young man.*
*Love, Grandma Geri*

Andy put the card down. He looked at this woman, and felt the bond of identity, magical and strange, that had long ago formed between them. She smiled. When their eyes met, she whispered "I love you," and then finished the rest of her tea. They were from the stars; they were of the same star. Grandma Geri stayed through breakfast, and after she left, his Uncle James called to say hello. The day wore on and it was peaceful. Later, his parents took him out to dinner to his favorite restaurant.

Andy never saw his grandmother alive again.

# Chapter Four

"She was driving in the car, according to the police." Mr. Mackpeace explained. "She had a stroke, lost control, and hit a tree. Grandma Geri died instantly. She never felt a thing."

It was the morning after his birthday. Andy sat at the same outdoor wooden table looking up at his father in complete shock. *This can't be happening. She was just here. She was sitting just here yesterday.* As he stared, the image of the man blurred as a gigantic tear rolled down Andy's face and went splat on his plate of eggs. His mother reached over and touched his head. She took his hand.

"Where was she going?" she asked.

"To the hotel. There was nobody else in the car."

Mr. Mackpeace squatted down next to Andy's chair and hugged him. "It's okay, Andy," he said. His father's body started to shake, and then, as if he were talking to himself, Mr. Mackpeace said in a sad, echo whisper, "It's okay, you can cry."

Andy stayed home from school the next day and spent most of the time in his room. He looked at some of his childhood scrapbooks and looked for pictures of Grandma Geri. There were the usual holiday group shots and birthday shots and Grandma Geri looked the same in every pose.

*She never gets any older.*

In a unique shot, Grandma Geri was stepping out of a roller coaster with complete ease and poise, like a model coming down a stairway.

One newspaper clipping, yellow with time, was wedged in among the pages. It was from the local paper dated 1957.

LOCAL GIRL MAKES GOOD ON BROADWAY!

The article described Grandma Geri's being in the chorus of a musical in New York City.

"First of several!" Grandma Geri liked to brag.

Andy smiled. He wished he could have seen her dance back then.

A different photo popped out from under some birthday cards. It was a picture, taken by his mother, of him and Grandma Geri in the middle of the labyrinth. They were outside in the woods, in Maine, and Grandma Geri had driven them far off the beaten path to find it.

Andy loved that labyrinth. The twists. The silence. When he had gotten to the middle, he didn't want to leave.

"It's so nice here," he whispered to his grandmother.

"This is how we want it to be in the whole world," she whispered back.

On the morning of the funeral, Andy wore a gray suit, the one his grandmother had given him for Christmas. "Dad, can you help me tie this?" he said as he walked into the bathroom carrying the golden silk necktie.

"You're getting taller," his father said standing behind him manipulating the tie with his hands. Andy tried to follow the motions, learn the steps, but got confused after the second turn. "Soon you'll have to start doing this on your own."

Andy smelled the toothpaste breath of his dad, the after shave, the pressure of his body as he breathed. Mr. Mackpeace finished the tie then wiggled the knot up toward the collar. Andy was tall like his father, given the same blond hair, the same thin build, yet Andy had his mother's blue eyes.

"Are you almost ready?" his father asked.

Andy looked in the mirror, adjusting the tie to make the knot tighter, his father's drained face behind him. Andy couldn't think of anything to say to make his dad feel better.

The family arrived at the funeral thirty minutes early, yet the tiny, small-town church was already filling up with people. Grandma Geri had lived most of her life in Silver Lake and had been a beloved woman.

"There's Uncle James," said Andy as a blue Volvo pulled into the parking lot. James got out of the car, said "hello" quietly to a few people, and came over to his family. He hugged Andy's mom, hugged his brother, and then, turned to Andy last. His hug was longer, and it seemed to Andy that his uncle was trying to infuse some sort of stability into his body.

When he stood back, James' eyes were wet. "Well," he said, as he motioned to the church. They walked together, across the gravel stones of the tiny lot toward the building.

The steps of the church were tiny and few, the church door was propped open by an old rock. When the Mackpeace family entered, and sat in the front row, the funeral began. No one remembered to shut the door, so the sunlight streamed in as one single ray, illuminating the carpeted foyer. It lingered there, like an angelic witness, a mystical grandmother who wanted to see this world one last time, and then say goodbye.

# Chapter Five

On the way home from the church, Andy rode with Uncle James. Andy was silent.

"Hey," Uncle James nudged him on the shoulder, "are you all right?"

"I can't think of anything to say."

"Who says you have to entertain me. What are you feeling right now?"

"I don't know. I know my stomach hurts. I just don't feel anything."

"Are you pissed off?" his uncle asked.

"No. What would I be pissed off about? I'm fine." Andy didn't want to continue this conversation. "What's going to happen to Grandma's ashes?" he asked.

Uncle James threw him a fast look and pulled the car into a bank parking lot. He shut off the engine and leaned back. "Talk to me. No bull."

Andy sat and stared out the window. Two women were coming out of the bank on their lunch hour, and as they crossed the street, the one woman was laughing. The other was relating a story and the woman was shrieking with laughter. He watched them walk into the sunlight and go into a restaurant. "Why do *they* get to laugh?" he asked. "Huh? Why?"

He pounded the seat with his fist. "Why did she die?" Andy smashed his fist into the seat again and again while the pain in his stomach became a fire. "What did she do that was so terrible? Who got to decide that she had to die?" His voice broke, and his face was hot with tears. "Why did you die, Grandma?" He pounded the seat harder, louder. Andy was embarrassed that his uncle was seeing him like this, but he just couldn't control himself. Snot flew out of his nose, and tears fell into his mouth, but he kept hitting the seat. "Why, huh? *Why*?"

Uncle James slid over and put his right arm around his nephew, his friend. Andy felt his arm and grabbed him with all his might. He smelled the dry cleaning fluids of his uncle's suit jacket, buried his face in the man's chest and cried. Uncle James didn't say a word.

Andy relaxed eventually; he stopped crying and lifted his head.

His uncle had tears in his eyes. He stroked Andy's hair. "It's totally okay to be mad at her," he said, his voice as soothing as a pool of water. "That's natural. Don't feel guilty about that. I don't know why she died, but it wasn't because she did something terrible, or that she somehow deserved it." Uncle James sighed. "I believe Grandma Geri knew when her time was up. And you miss her. You're grieving, Andy. Pound the seat, scream at the window, do whatever it takes to get it out. Because once you get it out, you move on."

Andy looked at the snot dripping down the front of Uncle James' suit. "I got it out all right." He reached into his pants for a Kleenex. "I'm sorry."

"Listen, Andy," James said as he stopped his nephew in mid air, "you don't ever say 'I'm sorry' around me, understand?" He pulled himself forward, wriggled out of the jacket, and threw it in the back seat. "It'll clean. It's fine."

"Okay."

"Now, are you ready to go home," as his uncle gestured to the cars parked in the bank lot, "or do you want to pummel the seats in those cars too?"

"No," Andy laughed and blew his nose. "I'm good."

"Well, if you get the urge, let me know. We'll find a used car dealer." Uncle James headed back to Andy's house.

Andy turned toward the window again, leaned his head against the pane and drifted off.

*Grandma Geri had worked at the two hotels overlooking the lake in the summer. During the day she taught Yoga and Jazz Dancing to the hotel guests; often, she stayed till late in the evening with her crystal ball doing her consultations. "What consultations?" Andy asked one night when she was home.*

*"People come to me," she said, "with questions about their lives, their dreams, but mainly about how to find their happiness. I consult them. The crystal ball helps me."*

*Whether she walked through a hotel lobby or the local supermarket, people stared at her. "You can't worry about what other people think of you," she said once. "I like to shake them out of their expectations."*

"She's going to have them scattered in the ocean, at Key West," Uncle James said.

"What?" Andy sat up and glanced over at his uncle.

"Her ashes. You asked me what the story was with her ashes. She's having them scattered over the water."

"When?"

"At sunset on December 21."

"The 21st? That's the Winter Solstice, right?"

"That's right. Grandma Geri loved to have a ritual on those special days. Of course, your father's not very comfortable with the idea. He's also not crazy about having to go somewhere as far as Key West."

"Why did Dad hate her funky clothes and her talking to the dead?"

Uncle James laughed. "Your father can be a really snooty professor! He didn't understand her all the time. He tried to box her into being a certain way: to be just a mom. That's one thing I learned fast with her, you couldn't box her in. You couldn't make her be this way or that way. She always was a free spirit. The sooner I accepted that about her, the easier it was for me to understand her."

"Didn't Dad love her?"

"Oh yeah, Andy, of course he did. But he was always hoping she would change; that she would just act 'normal'... whatever that means! But," Uncle James added, "and this is a big 'but,' he's slowly getting used to it, now that he sees a lot of Grandma Geri in you."

On Andy's bedroom wall was a poster Grandma Geri had given him last year for his birthday. It was a picture of a pond at dawn and under the picture it read:

"*Step to the beat of a different drummer,*
*no matter how distant or far away.*"

He didn't completely know what the quote meant, but he liked the idea of the words. He even overheard Grandma Geri saying that to his father when Andy was in bed.

"Mom, you have to stop influencing Andy, he's becoming a nervous wreck," he heard his father say one July night when the windows were open and the two adults were out on the patio.

"Andy's sensitive, Bill. He was born that way. He's very sensitive to the vibes he picks up from other people, from the pain he feels in the world."

"And that's going to put him in a hospital if he doesn't get a grip!" His father was beginning to lose his patience.

"Being sensitive has nothing to do with 'getting a grip,'" Grandma Geri said. "It's a gift; he could be an excellent psychic someday."

"There you go again! Will you stop trying to change him into something?"

"Your Andy steps to the beat of a different drummer, Bill," she had said while picking up the leftover drink glasses, blowing out the candle, and moving inside. "You remember that."

# Chapter Six

Days later, Andy dared to ask: "What about Grandma's crystal ball?" He was once again on the patio, and Andy's dad lowered his coffee cup. His face grew red and he sighed a very long sigh.

"Andy, *please* don't bring up the crystal ball. I don't want to talk about it. Your grandmother, as much as I loved her, was very odd sometimes. It's embarrassing for me that you even know about her crystal ball. I had hoped she threw that thing away."

That afternoon Andy, his parents, and Uncle James went to Grandma Geri's house to start organizing it and clearing out her personal things. The adults were in the kitchen.

"I found it!" Andy yelled from upstairs. Grandma Geri's house wasn't huge, just cluttered with costumes and candles and clothes and shoes. Hundreds of shoes! Grandma Geri even had a working water fountain in her living room. "The Crystal Ball!" Andy pronounced, as he brought it downstairs to his parents and his uncle who were sorting dishes. "It was in a hat box, in the 'Props Closet.'"

"So there's that old thing," Uncle James laughed. "I haven't seen that in about five years! I wonder if it still works." He took it out of Andy's hands and peered inside. "Looks like Auntie Em is worried about you, Dorothy. Better go home before you get into any more trouble."

"Jimmy, don't start!" Andy's dad said. "Take this

back upstairs and put it away. And look for those sets of keys I asked you about. Your grandmother was extremely absentminded. They could be any place." He gave the ball back to Andy and gave him a “no buts” look.

"Lighten up, Bill!" said Uncle James. "Maybe the ball knows where the keys are."

Uncle James and Andy walked upstairs to the affectionately named “Props Closet” and returned the crystal ball to its place. Andy loved this room. Grandma Geri kept all her psychic tools in here as well as her collection of mystical artifacts collected from around the world. The room was painted a light purple with blue trim and there was a small bay window peacefully set in a niche overlooking the back yard. A large armchair with a reading lamp was by it.

"This old 'Props Closet' was here even when I was little," Uncle James said. "I wasn't allowed in here by myself until I was thirteen. Your grandmother used it as some rite of passage or something with me."

"Grandma Geri took me in here when I was nine!" Andy boasted.

"Well," his uncle laughed. "Ain't you special!"

"And don't you forget it!"

On the floor were packs of picture cards and pie shaped charts. "What are these?" Andy asked shuffling through the cards and the funky papers. "I've seen these before, but I can't remember what Grandma told me."

"Those cards are called the Tarot, and the charts are astrology charts. Grandma Geri sometimes used them when consulting her clients."

A giant poster which read: "The Seven Chakras" was displayed on one wall. Hooded capes hung in the narrow closet near the window and scarves draped from the doorknob.

"I remember these!" Uncle James said, picking off one of the capes. "We weren't allowed to touch them. She used this red one every June 21: the Summer Solstice. She'd meet with her friends, and they'd go into the woods and bless the trees, bless the world."

Candles arranged by color were lying on four tall shelves. There were jars filled with oils: lavender and pine and eucalyptus. One table was arranged with little statues, authentic stones, and unpolished crystals. Andy fingered them as he thought about the times he spent in this room. A mobile consisting of coral, wood, and quartz *("Blessed by a Hawaiian kahuna," said Grandma Geri,)* glided effortlessly overhead in the quiet breeze.

"Well, would you look at this," Uncle James said as he picked up a photograph in a gold frame placed among the statues. "It's your grandmother; probably taken, oh, about twelve, fifteen years ago." In the photo, Grandma Geri was striking a dance pose. She was wearing a long skirt and delicate Chinese slippers. Her arms were extended and her long black hair was whirling behind her. Grandma Geri was looking toward the right, off into the distance. "She used to say that when she danced, she felt like a goddess. It was the closest thing to being immortal."

"She's beautiful," Andy said looking over his

uncle's shoulder at the photo.

"Your grandmother," Uncle James whispered, "was marvelous." He returned the photo to the table and moved toward the door. "She was one of a kind." He left Andy alone to search for the keys.

Andy took one more look around the room. On the floor under the window were different shaped boxes, including the hat box for the crystal ball. There was one small box with four tiny drawers attached to it. It was the perfect place to put a set of important keys.

Andy started with the smaller drawer and found a box of matches. He opened the long drawer and found something wrapped in tissue paper. He unfolded the paper carefully and laid the insides out on a table. They were incense sticks: long wands of incense, each a different color and smell. There were ten sticks all together.

The light outside was getting redder, the window overlooking the back garden was still open, but it was now a little cooler. Andy shut the window half way and went back to the incense. They were different colors: rust, yellow, blue, brown and he felt attracted to them. He had seen incense before, and sometimes he and his grandmother would light one and walk around the house with the smoke trailing behind them. He smiled at the thought. "Cleansing," Grandma had called it. "Good for your soul!"

"Have an intention whenever you light a candle or incense," she used to teach him, "or give a reason for your action."

Andy shut the door to the "Props Closet." He turned

back to the pile of sticks and picked out a ruddy, red one. He struck a match and brought the flame to the edge of the stick. The stick caught on fire and burned. Andy solemnly blew out the flame and immediately, the thick incense smoke wafted through the room.

He waved the smoking stick the way his grandmother had shown him, spanning from the ceiling to the floor, from one side to the other. "Good-bye Grandma," he said, gesturing North, South, East, and West. "I'll miss you, very much." The smoke was filling up the room. It had an orangey smell, sort of cinnamon, sort of apple, sort of cranberry. Andy brought the stick to his nose and took a big whiff. It smelled like Thanksgiving and pie and cold winter mornings.

Like the breath of a butterfly, the room disappeared. The walls simply dissolved. The roof lifted off, the walls melted into a fog and faded away. The floor turned into cobblestone, and Andy felt the uneven stones beneath his feet.

He was standing in the middle of a mud puddle.

# Chapter Seven

"Good night!" he said and jumped out of the water and onto the street. The room was gone. Andy was on the edge of a street in a foreign city. He stood there, his oddly shaped shoes soaking up the water from the tiny puddle. Men, women, some children were trudging through the streets, carrying lanterns for it was growing dark. There weren't any electric lights or cars. There wasn't anything recognizable. All the buildings had several chimneys blowing smoke from them, and the street lamps were little glass boxes with lighted candles.

What Andy saw and what he should be seeing didn't gel ... didn't compute. No "Props Closet," but there *should* have been a "Props Closet," He turned around half believing that Grandma Geri's house was simply behind him - and he marveled at his own lack of common sense. Andy was as confused and disoriented as if he had just stepped out of a tumbling dryer.

"What is this?" he asked himself. "What happened?"

Andy was cold. He stumbled away from this busy street and headed down a tiny, empty side street. At the far end of this smaller street Andy saw a park, and on the grass were hundreds of white, makeshift tents, like the kind he saw in pictures of refugee camps. Men were idling near the tents, sitting near campfires, talking. Andy smelled the strong salt air of the ocean. He heard cawing overhead and saw seagulls flying and landing on a house nearby. Bewildered, Andy stood still, blinked his eyes and shook his head.

"Get out of the road, you stupid article!" Two horseback riders galloped past him.

"What are you doing?" a boy around seventeen grabbed Andy's arm and pulled him over and out of the street. Andy put his extinguished incense stick into his coat pocket, a coat that was not his own. All the clothes he was wearing were not his own. His shirt was different, his pants, his boots, even his underwear! It was all different, heavy somehow, thick, itchy.

"What happened to me?" asked Andy.

"What do you mean, 'What happened to me?'" the stranger asked. "You almost got hit in the head by a horse. You can't see where you're going?"

"What's that smell?"

"Oh, I know, it's the troops on the Commons. Their latrine is a lousy hole and it stinks up the whole town. We're all bloody sick of it. The lobsterbacks are everywhere, telling us how to act, when to move, when to sit, like a dog, it is. I hear they're doing something about it. Had enough of it, I heard from the barber this morning."

"Barber?"

The incense stick had carried him off to another place. Andy couldn't figure out where, but that patch of green he saw was not a park. Something in his gut told him not to ask too many questions, he would find out in time. It wasn't summer anymore. It was more like a cold spring night, maybe late winter. There was a lot of snow still on the ground, but the sky was pinker since the sun was beginning to set. He *did* smell the ocean and he smelled the earth, slightly, above the smell of the latrine and the horses. It was that damp smell that soon told of spring.

He was trying to get a grasp on what had happened while figuring out how the heck he was going to get back to Grandma Geri's "Prop's Closet."

"Yeah, it's where me mate Garrick works all day, mate, He's apprentice to Shelton the Wigmaker, on Devonshire."

*Wigmaker? Devonshire, Devonshire ... .* Andy wanted to ask this lad what city he was in, but he held back. Something about witches, perhaps? He looked around again. The stores were closing up, and people were going home. Buildings of red brick and tall chimneys and narrow streets and cobblestone. Gosh, *where was he*??? London? The stranger next to him had a British accent, sort of. He was taller than Andy, thinner, gaunt even, like he had slept in a barn. His hair was thinning already and his beard was full. His left sleeve had several holes in it and he smelled like a fireplace.

"What do you keep looking around for? Are you waiting for somebody?"

"No," said Andy. "You look like something out of *Oliver Twist*."

"I don't know what you're talking about, but me name is Maverick, Samuel Maverick. I heard from the barber that nobody's taking any more of it. Last week was just the beginning. People are getting sick and tired of these lobsterbacks and..."

"Lobsterbacks! Got it! This is *Boston*! You're talking about the British!"

"Of course this is Boston, what else would it be? Where do you live?"

"I don't get out much," Andy said. His head was spinning. He'd been to Boston with his parents and Uncle James many times; it didn't look like the Boston he knew. The Commons, maybe, sort of, but there were no sidewalks, no gardens.

"Well me boy-o, come on with me. There's something going on down at the Customs House. I'm meeting me mates down there and I don't want to miss it." Samuel turned away from the smell on the Commons and headed up the street.

"Did the British fight at Concord yet? Paul Revere ride through Cambridge? What about the Boston Tea Party?" It just spilled out of Andy's mouth. He shut it, but it was too late.

Samuel stopped dead still. "What kind of witchcraft is you speaking lad? What kind of spy talk is this? Concord? Paul Revere? Do you talk to mock me? You think you can make fun of me and me mates and by God I should knock you down and beat you." He raised this suddenly very strong arm and swung it as hard as he could.

Andy ducked out of the way and ran to a wall in the darkness. "No, don't!" he cried. "I don't mean anyth ... I mean, I don't mean nothing. I just heard rumors of fighting and skirmishes and wondered if they were true. I want to participate ... I mean ... ." *Gosh*, he thought. *I've got to learn my history better. Obviously these haven't happened yet. What had happened first*?

*The tea dumping*? *Paul Revere*? *The Declaration of Independence was after that of course*, *but*, ***what year was it now***!?

"I want to help you drive off the lousy lobster scoundrels!"

"Well," said Samuel Maverick, "that's more like it me boy-o. Follow me, and you'll get a chance to see what we colonists do when we've been pushed around for too long." He grabbed Andy by the arm and pulled him down the street.

They walked for two blocks when a taller woman passed them. "Peter Anthony James Carey!" she said, going up to Andy with a smile of relief. "Your father's been looking for you. He said he'd wait for you at the Oyster House when you're ready to go. That was about half an hour ago." She moved on. "You don't want to keep him waiting too long: he's one for the pint if you know what I mean."

"I won't be long," he said. *Good night*! *Who was that*?

He tagged behind Samuel hoping Samuel would take him to the Oyster House later. He didn't know where else to go.

Not only did he not know where he was going, he didn't know where he was going to go *after* he went where he was going. The seriousness of his situation sank into his time-traveling soul.

# Chapter Eight

British soldier Hugh White was on sentry duty that day at the Customs House. It was March 5, and although Andy didn't know it, the year was 1770. It would be five years before Paul Revere and the Battle at Concord, three years before that impromptu Tea Party. By then, Hugh White would be stationed in Castle William in Boston Harbor. Later, after the war, he would return to England and remain in the King's service for the next fifteen years. But tonight, at 7:30, in this place not a stone's throw from the Boston Harbor, he had been doing sentry duty at the Customs House on Devonshire Street for the past four hours. He was cold and incredibly hungry. He was tired of the endless taunts.

"Wait til later, you piece of garbage!" It had started the moment he stepped outside. People going by said some awful things to him.

"You'd better not be here if you know what's good for you!" said one woman when she walked by with her husband.

They hated him. One young man even threw something unmentionable at him. It missed him, but Hugh had to not show any reaction, any emotion.

Hugh's job was to stand outside the Customs House for six hours and protect the British officials who worked inside it: a place piled with money to be sent to the King. The British workers throughout the city had asked for protection. The colonists were becoming unruly, so the King sent seven hundred soldiers. Seven hundred soldiers to be stationed around Boston. Seven hundred! "Good Lord!" said Hugh to a solder that morning. "I'm lucky enough to be in the barracks, but some of these men are out on the Commons in tents! Tents! In March, with snow still on the ground!"

Hugh was indeed lucky to be stationed down by the water. His job, too, could have been a lot worse: it was simply boring. Standing and standing and standing. His duty ended at 9:30 where then, he could go back to the barracks and eat with his mates and go to sleep. Hugh was tired. His right shoulder ached from the constant stress of eyeing the people walking by. Did someone have a gun? Was someone going to attack the building? Boston had become the worst town in all the colonies to police. Worse than New York. Worse than Philadelphia even, that's what Tom Doty, another soldier, had told him.

Bells started to ring in a nearby church. The bells rang whenever there was a fire nearby. It was a signal for people to run out and help. "But I don't smell any smoke," Hugh said to himself.

The week before had been really tense. People all over the city were picking fights with soldiers. Soldiers walking down the street even, just walking, had snowballs thrown at them and people spitting on them. On Water Street, two girls, about eight years old, accosted a soldier returning home to his barracks. "Here he comes," their mother had whispered to them. The two angels walked outside and innocently strolled in his direction. As they came even with the unsuspecting soldier, the two girls threw off the wooden lid of a small pail. Before he could even defend himself, they hurled the bucket at his head. When it struck, warm, sour, five day old milk ran down his hair, his face and his uniform.

"Go jump in the ocean, you slimy lobster!" the girls yelled. They ran back into their home screaming as if the soldier had been chasing them. The frightened man came in through the barracks door reeking of the milk and was ordered to take a hot bath.

"Where did eight-year-old girls learn to hate so much?" Hugh had said to the soldier. "We're trying to keep peace here. We're trying to prevent chaos from happening."

But now, at 7:30, on this cold Monday night, the ebb and flow of the crowds in his vision began to slow down. People were not just walking to somewhere, they were walking to here. Men, women, boys, many boys, were starting to group up and were staring at him.

"Hey, Lobsterback, you lousy piece of slime! I'm talking to you!"

One boy, around seventeen, started heading toward Hugh. He had blond hair that was tucked back behind his ears. The boy's legs never stopped moving, and he kept his eyes on Hugh the entire time. Two younger boys behind this upstart were bending over making a pile of snowballs. Hugh kept silent. Most of the trouble starts when a soldier answers back.

"That's what they want you to do," Hugh's commanding officer had always warned Hugh. "They know they've irritated you when you start to answer them back."

Hugh stayed silent and watched as the crowd started to grow. The bell ringing became insistent, like a giant call to arms.

"I said, I was *talking* to you!" The slovenly dressed youth yelled. "Why don't you get out of here? *Go home*! *Huh*? When are you filthy, stinking, sons of dogs going to get out of our town?"

Hugh's back stiffened. His hair stood up on the back of his neck. This was getting serious. He was cold and hungry and he was fed up with the lack of respect. The rage in his stomach grew into a ball of heat that started to move throughout his body.

The crowd grew larger.

Larger.

The insulting boy was getting closer and closer to Hugh and if Hugh didn't do or say something, the boy would be able to touch him. "You," the boy said.

"Was he drunk?" Hugh wondered.

"You're nothing but a puppet for the king. 'Yes, your Majesty; of course, your Majesty,'" he began prancing around imitating a marionette. Hugh saw the stubble on the boy's face, he was that near. The crowd laughed and urged the boy on. "You dog!" the boy growled. "You swine! You're nothing! You can't do anything! You -"

Hugh smacked the boy across the left side of his head with the butt of his musket. The boy's face was a complete "O" as it hit the snow. He rolled over onto his side and his hand flew up to his head to see if he was bleeding. He wasn't.

"*That's enough*!" Hugh roared.

The crowd was instantly silent. The young rebel got up, staggered back into the crowd, and ran off. Hugh took that moment to rush into the Customs House and summoned John Preston, the British officer on duty.

"Sir," he yelled. "Quick! Those people are becoming ... it's serious. There are about three hundred of them out there, and they're not going away! I must have back up!"

Preston and six other men went outside with Hugh. Their muskets were not loaded. Their bayonets were attached.

"OOOOOOOOO!" the crowd laughed when the soldiers reappeared.

"Look who has to get reinforcements when one boy calls him names!" said a woman. The crowd had swelled. They were standing in semi-circles around the soldiers, at least six to seven rows deep. At this time, joining the last circle, came Andy and Samuel.

# CHAPTER NINE

"I told you something was up!" Samuel said. "We're going to show these...!" A bell drowned out his last word. He grabbed Andy and moved up through the ranks of the crowd toward the front. "You lobster scum! *Go home*!"

"Stop grabbing me!" Andy said. Something was wrong here. He could feel it.

Grandma Geri always encouraged him when he had those feelings. "Trust your gut" was her crude but accurate description. "Andy," she'd say, "there are energy forces in this earth that we cannot see, but they are here. They help us, not hurt us. So when you feel your gut telling you that something is weird, or off, or something unexpected is about to happen, *Listen to it*! Remember Andy: 'There are more things in heaven and earth, Horatio, than are dreamt of in your philosophy.'"

She smiled. "That's Shakespeare, not me."

A voice from the back yelled out. "That's the son of a dog that knocked me down!"

Andy turned and saw a blond haired boy with a huge torch standing on top of some stairs and pointing at a British soldier. He held a snowball, and hurled it at the soldiers. It hit the wall over their heads. The ball exploded and two sharp rocks flew out of it and landed on the ground.

"Load your muskets, but do not fire," Preston said. The other soldiers begrudgingly did what they were told. "I repeat, do not fire unless I say so."

"I'd like to kill the whole lot of them," one soldier said.

"Go ahead!" said one woman who overheard the exchange. "I dare you!"

Samuel joined in. "Yeah, go ahead, I dare you. Fire! I dare you! You lazy cowards!" He scooped up a clump of snow, made a ball and hit a soldier right in the face.

The crowd of men and boys and those few women grew bigger. Louder. They edged closer to the small group of soldiers. Andy felt the people pressing and knew this crowd could easily overtake the small band of militia.

"Go ahead, I dare you! Fire!"

"Fire, though you dare not!"

"You lobster scoundrels! You rascals!"

The colonists seethed. Their courage increased for they had had enough. Enough badgering and enough bullying. They too were cold and tired and hungry. But above all, they hated. They hated these British people who bossed them around. They hated these British rules and these British blockades. They couldn't see anything else but that hatred. Some had clubs and pieces of wood. A group of boys threw more snowballs.

"Steady men, I say, keep an eye on them and don't fire!" warned Preston. "We'll see how far this will go. They may just get tired and go home. Don't talk back to them. Don't encourage them."

Andy watched as more boys gathered and pitched the rock-laden snowballs.

Snowballs.

*I've seen this before. In history class. Snowballs ... snow and crowds and ... .*

His stomach lurched. He knew what this was! It was 1770. This was the Boston Massacre.

Massacre!

Andy grabbed Samuel's arm and pulled him hard. "Get out of here. You have to get out of here. This is dangerous. They're going to start shooting!" he screamed.

"Don't be an ass! They're not going to do anything," Samuel pushed back. He joined the crowd in their taunts. "I dare you! Fire! Go ahead, Fire!" He threw a brick, and then more snowballs with rocks in them. "*Fire*!"

The crowd grew braver and began throwing harder objects at the soldiers. The noise was louder and louder. Andy tried again. He screamed at Samuel. "We have to get *out* of here! I'm serious!"

"Stop grabbing me!" Samuel yelled. He pushed Andy who fell down onto the feet of the people behind him. Then one of the soldiers (and we know it was one of two), heard the word "*Fire*!", mistook it as an order from Preston, and pulled the trigger.

Samuel's stomach exploded with blood. The bullet continued through his body, out his back, and into the leg of a heavy man standing behind him. That man fell on top of Andy and started screaming. More shots rang out. People ran and bumped into each other and fell down. The noise of the guns blasting in that small street was unnerving. It was like the sound of a war.

Andy was pinned beneath the man with the hurt leg who for obvious reasons did not get back up again. Andy watched as a man attacked Preston and beat him with a club. Another man was running away when two bullets hit him in the back. The man never felt a thing. One ball had gone through his chest. It hit his heart. One minute he was breathing cold, noisome sea air, and the next minute, dead.

"Not now," Andy muttered. "Please, not now. Get me out of here." The left side of his face was flat in the snow. He saw boots running and people storming and bodies lying still. The cold snow made his cheek burn, but he didn't move. "Stay still," he said to himself. "They won't see you if you stay still."

The shooting lasted two minutes; for Andy it felt like two years. Those loud muskets that boomed into his ear and created this nightmare. Around him were the sounds of crunching boots on snow and crying and moans.

Suddenly, the shooting stopped.

Dead silence. Andy heard the water lapping near a boat. People cautiously returned to check on friends who had been shot or trampled. Some were dead and others wounded. Andy wriggled out from under the wounded man and looked over at Samuel.

When the bullet hit the lad, all his inner muscles lost control and he instantly defecated. Urine, too, stained his pants. Samuel was on the ground holding where his stomach had been. The blood was oozing through his fingers and splashing on the snow. Two men picked him up and carried him into a building nearby. The soldiers, too, were gone. Andy never saw Samuel again.

Samuel Maverick would die the next day and be buried with the others in the Granary Burial Grounds.

Andy's head got very light. The sharpness of the world became fuzzy and he stumbled away from the scene. His stomach churned within him. The pain was so intense he thought he too had been shot. He was going to be sick, so he ran over to an alley and threw up.

He wiped his mouth and staggered around in a circle. He was shaking and crying. It was really getting dark; he was in a strange city in another time and he didn't know what to do next. The pains in his stomach were unbearable. He leaned against the brick wall and held his stomach. He slid down the side of the wall and folded up into a fetal position.

Grandma Geri used to tell him it was okay to feel so afraid. "Get the pain out and then you will know what to do," she said.

Andy felt a small hand on his back. He jumped. A woman bent over him. "Are you cold?" she asked. "Come down here: there is a fire for you."

Andy stood up, wiped his eyes and followed the woman down the alley. At the other end, around the corner, he saw a makeshift fire and shadows. Some very poor people were standing around it and talking about what had happened.

"It's the beginning of something big, I can feel it!" said one.

"They're never going to leave. They'll stay until

we're all dead."

Now whether it was the intervention of Grandma Geri, or simply that the pain now was out of him, Andy started to think. He saw the fire, and the smells of the smoke, which triggered him to think about the incense.

*If the incense got me here, maybe it will get me back.*

The stick, due to the fighting, pushing and pinning, had broken into many small pieces. Using his fingers, Andy felt in his pocket for the longest one. He didn't want the other people to see him comparing and analyzing pieces of incense! He had forgotten how easily superstitious the people were around here. He pulled it out and slid the piece slowly toward the fire, trying to remain nonchalant.

"What's *that*?" someone yelled. Andy jumped so much that he almost dropped the stick. The woman who yelled was pointing into the fire at the tiny fragment of stick. "What are you doing?"

The stick caught fire. The smoke started to swirl, and in the open air, it swirled away from Andy and toward the open sky.

"He's got something!"

Someone grabbed his arm. Andy quickly yanked it toward his face and inhaled with every ounce of strength in his body.

*If this doesn't work, I'm toast.*

The fire was the first to disappear. The gnarly hand grabbing him was the last. It all sort of evaporated. No sounds of screams or "I'm melting! I'm melting;" everything simply faded away.

Andy was back in the “Props Closet.”

It was summer. He had on his own clothes: the shorts and the blue T-shirt. The cooler smells of flowers and grass came through the window. Andy was standing just as before. His cheek wasn't sore, and there was no splattered blood on his arms or legs from the shootings. He checked his hair, his head, his body for signs of twigs or snow or dirt or anything that said, "I just went back in time." There was nothing.

"It's not real, I'm back." He laughed with relief. "It was real. But I'm back. I'm nuts. I've inherited Grandma Geri's nuttiness."

Then he looked up and saw the keys. The missing Grandma Geri keys. They were on a huge ring, right in plain sight, sitting on the doorknob of the little closet. The incense sticks were lying in their case, untouched.

"What are you up to up there, Grandma?" he said. "You're seeing me right now, I can feel it." He shut the drawer and put it off to the side. He found an old baby blanket and threw it over it. Somehow, he would sneak that drawer into his own bedroom back in his home.

And somehow, Roger would have to know about this. And maybe Miranda.

But first Roger. Roger might be able to explain this.

Andy walked out of the room and headed down the stairs. "I found them!" he yelled, the keys jingling in his right hand.

# CHAPTER TEN

"Massacre, Andy? *The Boston Massacre*?" Roger Stanley was sitting in Andy's room two days later. Andy *finally* was able to tell him about his adventure in a place where there was privacy and time.

"*Yesss*!" Andy insisted. "*The* Boston Massacre! I was talking to Samuel Maverick himself! He's buried in the Granary: he's one of the famous five!"

"What about Crispus Attucks? Did you see him?" Roger was always looking at everything from the black perspective. "I did a report on him in fourth grade during Black History Month."

"Roger, there were hundreds of people there, and *no*, I didn't see Crispus Attucks. Hello! I don't even know what he looks like! There were several black people around." Andy gave up. "I know this is hard to believe, I know you think I'm whacked. But I was there, Roger. Somehow, through Grandma Geri's weird incense sticks, I *was there*."

Roger Stanley was Andy's best friend. They had been best friends ever since fourth grade when Ronnie Thurman had beaten Andy up. It was in the playground, behind the pine trees and out of sight of the teachers. Ronnie was hitting Andy and pushing him to the ground when Roger stepped in. He grabbed Ronnie Thurman's arm and whirled him around backwards, and Ronnie fell down on a tree stump. "Knock it off, Ronnie," he threatened. "Leave him alone, or else you'll have to fight me!"

Andy had been embarrassed and relieved all at the same time. He was frightened of Ronnie and glad Roger had saved him. Yet, he was angry with himself for letting Ronnie pick on him. "Why can't I stand up to Ronnie by myself?" Ronnie Thurman never touched him again, and Andy and Roger hung out together every day.

"Maybe the sticks are a hallucinogen," offered Roger. "Maybe they're like Magic Mushrooms or Peyote or something. They trip you out, and you *dream* about some event. Your dream is so real that you wake up and swear it really happened. That can explain why there's no trace of anything on your clothes. You were asleep!"

"Roger, I smelled the latrine. I smelled the sea. I smelled the gunpowder and the blood. I *smelled* it. When my face hit the ground, that ground was cold! You can't forget the feeling of cold snow pressed against your face. I don't just swear that they were real, they *were real*!"

"If you're so plucked by this, then why did you keep the sticks? Why didn't you throw them away or tell your Dad?"

"I don't know. I wanted to be sure that I'm not crazy. Maybe you're right, it's a hallucinogen. Or maybe it's no different than some 3-D ride at Disney World. Remember the one that freaked me out so much I had to sit in the shade for ten minutes? The sticks have the ability to create this illusion of a particular time in history. Grandma Geri has tons of weird things in the "Props Closet." She collected them from all over the world. This is just one of them."

Andy waited as Roger sat thinking. He trusted Roger because Roger always knew when he was nervous, or upset, or angry, and Andy didn't even have to say a word.

Andy's eyes were a little wild, and his lips were trembling.

"All right," said Roger finally. "Something happened to you; so, what do you want to do about it?"

"Prove it one way or the other. Go with me," Andy said. "Pick another one, light it, and see where it goes. Or rather, see where it takes us."

"Good night, look at the time," Roger feigned a look at his watch. "White people sure know how to keep a guy engaged!"

"C'mon Roger," coaxed Andy. "What have you got to lose? It's just a dream you said, it's not real. Well," he offered Roger a selection of incense sticks, "here's your chance to find out."

"You mean, by myself?"

"No! I'm going with you. I've got matches and a compass and since we have the stick, we're fine. I'll make you a deal: If the incense really and truly takes us to another time, cool. So be it. The moment you start to feel uncomfortable, or scared or whatever, you say the word. I mean it. We'll light the stick again, sniff it, and we're back. No discussion. No guilt trip. No judgments. Whaddya say?"

Andy knew Roger was curious but starting to feel scared. Roger looked at the sticks, their different colors and their various smells wafting through the room.

He hesitated. "I'm not a coward," he said.

"I know you're not," Andy said. "I wouldn't think any less of you if you backed out. I just want to see if it's real or not. I want you to verify that by going with me."

"What if we end up in Ancient Rome? The Coliseum? The sinking of the Titanic?"

"What if we end up in Hawaii? King Kamehameha? The Hanging Gardens of Babylon?"

"Andy, the glass isn't always half full."

"Sure it is. Now pick. Pick out whatever stick you wish, it'll be your choice. I'll light it and together we'll whiff."

Roger peered into Andy's hand and picked out a brown stick.

Andy smiled. "I should have figured."

"Brown is beautiful, old friend."

Andy took the stick from Roger and held it up. It looked perfectly natural and normal. It wasn't shaking or vibrating or making any bizarre sounds like a wand does in a movie. Andy pulled out the matches he had found at Grandma Geri's, and he and Roger scrunched closer together. No one was home downstairs, and the entire house was quiet. Andy had planned it that way. It was the best way to talk to Roger: without interruptions.

The house, unfortunately, was too quiet. There was no one to greet Miranda Roberts when she came to the front door. No one said "Hello!" to her after she knocked once and opened the door. Andy and Roger's muffled voices were coming from the open upstairs window.

She nonchalantly let herself in and climbed the stairs. Andy heard nothing when she walked down the hall toward his bedroom like she had a zillion times before.

Miranda threw open the door and yelled, "Freeze! What are you two *doing* up here?"

At that very moment, Andy and Roger were inhaling the thick aroma flavor of the incense smoke. It smelled somewhat sweet, somewhat earthy. It smelled of a flavor Andy had tasted before but couldn't remember. The room was swirling with smoke when Miranda burst in on them. Andy, at the surprise, consequently dropped the stick, the matches, and the compass.

Miranda's puzzled face was the last thing he saw before the walls dissolved, the bedroom disappeared and all three of them landed with a grunt on a riverbank in a field of tall grass.

It was there that a rattlesnake bit Andy on his right leg, just below the knee.

# CHAPTER ELEVEN

"Good night!" yelled Andy. The snake was ready to strike again, so Andy started crawling backward up the hill like some bizarre gym class exercise from first grade. Miranda grabbed an old fat branch lying nearby. Three years of field hockey had made her quite an accomplished player. Andy kept his eyes on the snake and just as it was about to bite him again, Miranda sent it flying through the air with a WHACK! of her stick. It landed on the other side of the little creek they were near and crawled off in a daze.

"It bit me!" Andy said. "It *bit* me! I can't believe this!" Roger hunkered over his friend and then knelt down next to the bite. It was small. "Your clothes are loose fitting," Roger explained. "It couldn't sink its teeth in you very far."

"Now how would *you* know?" Andy barked. "What do you know about snakes?"

"I don't know," Roger admitted. "I just do. I hate snakes. I've never read about them or studied them. But I know." He took a sharp little rock out of the ground and rolling up Andy's pant leg, he slashed a line across the bite in Andy's leg.

"Ouch!" his friend yelled. "Get away from me!"

Roger grabbed Andy's leg, and sucked as hard as he could where the line intersected the bite. Blood came to the surface, and Roger spat it out on the ground. He did it again, and again.

"I've only seen that in movies," said Miranda. "But

I don't think that's safe." She was wearing this huge, uncomfortable dress that hung all over her. The shock of the snake was beginning to wear thin and she, for the first time, looked around her.

"Where are we?" she asked "What happened to your bedroom?"

Andy didn't answer her. He was staring at Roger. "What are you doing?"

"I'm sucking out the poison until you get help," Roger explained. "The cut I made forces the area to bleed and that's where the poison is: in the bloodstream. I'm getting it out before it travels too far." He pulled a small handkerchief from his dirty pants and tied it as hard as he could just above the wound.

"You're never supposed to do that!" Andy said. "You're supposed to use one of those poison vacuum thingies." Andy was dumbfounded. *What's Miranda doing here*? *Where were they*?

"I don't know how I know to do this," said Roger, "I just do. It's second nature or something. But what I'm worried about is that you need a doctor. We have to get this looked at. People have died from rattlesnake bites. Andy, you said that if I feel scared, we would go back. Well, this bite is serious, I am scared. Let's go back. If the bite is still real, we can go to the hospital back home."

"We can't Roger. I dropped the stick. It's in the bedroom. When Miranda came in, I was so surprised that I dropped everything: the matches, the compass, the stick. I'm sorry. I-"

"*What do you think you are doing*?!"

The three adventurers jumped and looked up the hillside. There, at the top was a large black man with a straw hat. "If Moxley ever caught you with these two, you'd be dead! I've been looking for you for ten minutes! Get back to work before anyone sees you!"

Roger stood up. He knew the man was talking to him. The look in the eyes, the simple language, it was all encoded with hidden meaning. A large gap suddenly appeared between being white and being black. "Yes sir, I was helping the boy. He was bit by a rattler."

"Master Drew bit? When?"

"Just now. I started to suck the poison out when you came over the hill. I think he needs a doctor."

"I'll take him back. You go over to the field and finish the picking. Steven will tell you which group to go to."

Andy intervened, "But he has to stay with us! He saved my life." All the while this was happening Andy kept thinking: *Okay, where are we? Where are we? America? Of course. The speech patterns, the fields. Master Drew? It was hot here. Summer, late summer? August maybe? Humid too.* He looked at his clothes. He had on short trousers and a plain, white buttoned shirt. He was wearing thin shoes and no socks. *What year is this?*

He looked at Miranda who was sinking into her white clothes with confused resignation. Since she was sitting, she tried to shift the material around and all it did was make her more entangled. It engulfed her. She too had on thin shoes, and also a bonnet tied around her head. Or should have been. In her field hockey moment, it had lurched off of her and hung down her back.

All Andy kept hearing in his head was “Master Drew.”

*Oh no, it can't be.*

Roger said, "I can't leave my friend, he's ... .”

"*What did you say*?" the towering man took two steps toward Roger. "Get ... up ... ! and *go*!"

Roger ran up the hill to where the man was pointing. He didn't have a choice. When he edged over the crest, he stopped dead in his tracks. His mouth popped open and he swore under his breath.

A giant, living, breathing, working plantation spread out before him. Fields of cotton and corn, sweet potatoes and sugar cane. *Cotton*! Rows and rows and rows of white laid out like a giant white blanket over the earth. People everywhere in the fields: picking, harvesting. All black people. Even children. Not a tractor or a car or a truck. Horses and wagons were under some trees far to the left. Down beyond all of this, past a stream, a duck pond, some more buildings, Roger saw the main house. A beautiful plantation house Roger had only seen in pictures when he studied this in history class.

*I'm a slave. That's why I knew the secret behind that man's words. He was trying to protect me. I'm a piece of property.*

"Rufus! Get over here, child," a woman yelled to Roger. "Moxley is coming back after dinner with the Master. We require help here."

Roger headed in her direction. She was standing

with a group of other women all with large, empty baskets. It looked like they had just finished eating, because they were walking out of the grove of trees and the shade and into the bean rows. They lined up in a row about eight feet apart and started to pick beans in rhythm. Roger took the extra basket and joined in. He worked with the women, three teenaged girls, and two boys about his age.

*I'm living it. I took one sniff of a piece of incense and now I'm stuck here*. He picked the beans fast and furious. "Damn you, Andy!" he said.

"Quiet Rufus! Do your work and no talking!" the lead woman reprimanded. "We don't want any more punishments from Moxley. Look what happened to your sister."

Back at the riverbank, the tall man started down the hill toward the two very confused companions.

"What's going on, Andy!" said Miranda under her breath. "What happened to us?"

"I'll tell you later!" Andy whispered back. "Just play along."

"Play at *what*!" Miranda was furious. "I'm dressed up like Scarlett O'Hara!"

"Well, it's a place to start ... ." Andy smirked as the man arrived. He picked up Andy and headed back up the hill.

"I'll carry you, Master Drew. Don't want that poison to travel any more than it can. Miss Nancy will fix it. Do you want me to send for a horse, Miss Miriam?"

Miranda didn't answer. Miranda was struggling to walk in this ridiculous get-up in this awful, hot sun and the bonnet kept hitting the back of her neck.

"That's *you*!" Andy whispered to her. "Say something."

"What!" she said.

"The horse, Miss Miriam." The man was patiently looking at her. "Do you want me to send for a horse to take you home?"

"I think it'll take more than a horse to get me home," she said.

Andy gave her a look over the man's shoulders. “Play it cool,” it said. “Careful! Don't get sore now!”

"I can walk," Miranda said.

When they got to the top of the hill, Andy and Miranda, like Roger before, gasped at what they saw. Andy's suspicions were becoming more and more actualized. Andy learned, from his experience in Boston, that the best way to survive was to keep quiet and *think*! And listen!

The three traveled past all the long fields lit by the blazing sun and over the bridge of the little stream. The white plantation house was partially in shade at this time of the day. There were orchards on the left side of it and small children playing under the trees. Tinier buildings were within walking distance of the Main House. There was a well and next to that, a large bell which hung on a rafter.

On the far right, Andy and Miranda saw dilapidated shacks made of logs. They were close together, and there were little gardens and woodpiles adjacent to each one of them. On the far left, they saw a dark, dank cemetery with a few trees interspersed in it.

Before they got to the mansion, the man stopped. "This is as far as I am allowed to go," he said. He put Andy down and waved to a black woman working in the herb garden. "Get Miss Nancy! Her boy's been bit by a rattler."

"Who are you telling to 'get!'" She stared at the man with pure venom. "You get bak to the field. You're not supposed to come in here unless you're told! Field trash!"

"What's going on?" whispered Miranda.

"She's a house slave," said Andy. "They always thought of themselves as better than field slaves."

"Slaves? There aren't any slaves anymore. There haven't been slaves since Lincoln freed them in 1862."

"Well, this ain't 1862," Andy said, as a foreboding looking man in a dark hat came onto the porch, "and that sure as heck ain't Abraham Lincoln."

# Chapter Twelve

Andy, Roger, and Miranda had landed at Glendower, a 3,200-acre plantation estate in the southernmost part of Georgia. The foreboding man on the porch was John Finlayson and he, with his wife Nancy, owned the farm and 250 people.

The plantation grew acres of cotton and sweet potatoes, beans, corn, blueberries, sugar cane, and pecans. It was a massive-running institution. There were ducks and hogs; cattle, chickens, and horses. There was a hen house and a smoke house and a well. A springhouse was built over the cold creek that ran through the property. Inside, on dark shelves, were stored hams, meats, milk, and other items that required a cooler temperature. It was their way of having a refrigerator.

The plantation had a white overseer named Moxley. Moxley was a strong, muscled man who was not very tall. His dark, hairy arms and hands combined with his solid, dark eyebrows gave him the look of a pit bull.

Every morning this monstrous overseer gave orders to the slaves about whatever farming duties required the most attention. Every morning he counted the slaves: who was sick, who had run away and had to be tracked down, and who was pregnant. He wrote everything in a journal so that John Finlayson, the master, could keep track of all his property. Moxley oversaw the planting, the hoeing, the harvesting, and the marketing. He was not well educated with formal schooling but had a good sense with numbers. When it came to knowledge about crops and planting, he was brilliant; he was one of the most respected and feared overseers in the state.

Yet, above all, Moxley despised slaves, and he was trapped by his hatred. He looked at them with disgust and only saw them as animals. Living farm animals. His salary was based on how much cotton and other goods were sold to the markets. The more he sold, the more money he made. To get more crops, he made the slaves do more work: faster, sooner.

"Ask Mr. Moxley to come to the Main House," ordered Mr. Finlayson to the field slave who had carried Andy. "Petunia," he said to the house slave who had interrupted the carrying, "Go find Miss Nancy and ask her to come: Master Drew is ill."

Miranda watched the proceedings like a fish in a new tank. Nothing made sense. People were speaking English and responding to orders, but the circumstances were beyond her comprehension. Miranda Roberts prided herself on her ability to put confusing situations to rights. She could easily resolve a complex-looking word problem in math class, and her skill at finding information on the Internet was a credit to her classmates.

This, this world, however, didn't make any sense. She had been pitched overboard out of some canoe in a fast moving river. She couldn't grab the canoe, so she floated downstream as it swept her along. She looked around some more to try to find her grounding.

Up on the hill she saw a molasses gin. Near that was a grist mill (since it looked like something she had seen in a history book) for turning wheat into flour, and, next to that, although she didn't recognize it, was a cotton gin.

Miranda saw Petunia, the woman who had been working in the garden, run into a smaller building adjacent to the main house. Several herbs were hanging and drying near the door. Inside, people were cooking and baking.

*Okay*, Miranda thought. *This has to be some movie set, or one of those "living history" places where they run around in real costumes and recreate some life of the past. What else can this be*?

Miranda wanted to scream in frustration.

That smaller building was the kitchen; at Glendower and at all the plantations in the South, the kitchen was separated from the Main House. This prevented the Main House from catching fire or getting too hot from all the cooking.

These kitchens were very self-sufficient with their own herb and vegetable gardens right nearby. The herbs were used for cooking, and since doctors and knowledge of medicine were rare, most folks used herbs for healing. Miss Nancy, Andy and Miranda's, or rather, Drew and Miriam's mother, was the chief "doctor" of the place. She knew the remedy for any disease and had the ingredients and the herbs to make whatever tea or plaster that was required.

Miss Nancy appeared in the kitchen door. She was accompanied by a well dressed slave looking rather like a butler.

"James," she ordered touching the man on the arm.

"Attend to Master Drew, and take him to his bedroom."

Miss Nancy was not very tall, but exceedingly healthy. She would outlive her husband by twenty years. She was thin and energetic. Practical. Bossy, but extremely efficient. She oversaw the entire run of the household: the cleaning, the sewing, the cooking, the entertaining and the making of all the clothes.

She was in charge of keeping the inventory for the slaves' clothes up to date. Each year she measured every slave and fitted him or her properly with the correctly measured clothing. This clothing was never bought. She, or rather, her house slaves as well as Miriam, *made* each of the clothes: spun the cotton into thread, dyed it, and then weaved it into jeans and shirts and dresses all sewn by hand. Miss Nancy never wasted her time.

"Yes, Ma'am," James said and walked over to Andy and scooped him up.

"I can walk," said Andy who was getting annoyed at all the bossing around and this subservient behavior.

"Nonsense!" Miss Nancy said. "Petunia told me you were bitten by a rattler, and the worst thing you can do is start walking on that leg. James! To his bedroom." Miss Nancy exited through the kitchen in search of the correct herbs for snakebite.

"Yes, Ma'am," James said again. He carried Andy up the steep white stairs to the front porch, through the main doors, and continued up the main stairway. Andy watched his face for any signs of fatigue or stopping. James was a slim man about thirty-five years old,

Andy guessed, and he didn't seem bothered by carrying a thirteen-year-old boy up several flights of stairs.

Andy was wrong. James was bothered. All the slaves were bothered. There was nothing they could do or say to change their work-laden lives.

Andy's snakebite was getting worse. Half way up the stairs to the second floor, Andy's eyes wouldn't stay focused. He shook his head to make his eyes sharpen, but the walls started to spin. He passed out for a few minutes, then woke up, alone, in a small, four poster bed. He stared out the huge window overlooking the main road. He saw two wagons filled with corn pulled by mules crawl slowly down the road from the fields. Two slaves were driving the mules and trailing behind to pick up any corn that might fall off, were four slave children. Walking.

Plantation houses were built high off the ground to keep away the damp, the bugs, the snakes, the diseases. Andy was on the second floor. Miss Nancy came in, gave him some quinine water and wrapped his leg where the fang marks were with some herbs and something hot.

"Sleep now," she said. "You're a little weak, but you'll be fine."

Miranda had not been allowed to watch Andy being taken care of.

"Go back downstairs, you," ordered Miss Nancy. "It is not proper for you to be in here."

Miranda did what she was told, but sitting alone in a stuffy living room tried her patience. She walked around trying out the chairs and touching the desks and the mantles. The chairs were straight backed and little. It was like one of those replica rooms in a museum with the red rope stretched across the doorway so no one could walk in it. Yet, she walked in it. After an hour, when all the footsteps and commotion upstairs finally died away, Miranda crept out of the parlor, snuck up the main staircase, and headed for Andy's closed bedroom door.

Meanwhile, Andy had to go to the bathroom. Since he couldn't walk to the outhouse, and they didn't have indoor plumbing, he used a small bowl which was then placed in a special cabinet for the house slave to empty at a later time. Miranda walked in just as he was setting the bowl inside the cabinet. He nearly dropped it all over the floor.

"Good night! Don't you ever knock?"

"Sorry," she said, looking at the bowl. "I forgot about that part." She closed the door. Andy hopped into the bed and put the blankets around him even though it was 97 degrees outside. The house was cool, and the fever made him chilled.

"Are you going to be all right?" she asked.

"Yes, apparently I am. The bite wasn't that fierce, and the venom didn't affect me as much as it should have. I think all I'm supposed to do is just lie here and sleep for a while. I should be fine in a few hours."

Miranda looked him in the eye, and with a voice that would make her field hockey captain in three years said, "Andy, what's going on? Where are we?"

"I don't exactly know," he stammered. "But I do know that the Civil War hasn't happened yet."

"Sure it did. It happened over 140 years ago."

Andy nodded his head in the direction of the outdoors. "Not to them it hasn't. Miranda, we're back in time. I just don't know what time. It's Grandma Geri's incense sticks. I found them in her house and whenever I light one, it sends me back as a real person into a real place in time. Roger and I were lighting one to go on an adventure when you walked in on us in my room, remember? Well, you too got a whiff of the incense, and whoever sniffs it..." he gestured into the air, "gets whisked off."

Miranda looked at him like he was the two-headed sheep at the state fair. "We got whisked off? To where?"

"I haven't figured that out yet. The last time I sniffed one, I got shot back to the Boston Massacre in 1770, I was some guy named Peter Carey, but it took me awhile to figure all that out. You just can't go up to somebody and say, 'Hi! I'm from another place and time: by the way, what year is it, oh, and if you don't mind, where am I? and oh, one more, *who* am I?' If you keep quiet, and listen, you'll get the information."

Miranda collapsed into a nearby chair and her big, lumpy dress fell around her.

"This isn't the snakebite talking," he continued. "I'm not on any painkiller or anything. It's surreal, I agree."

Andy knew that practical Miranda couldn't adjust to changes very easily. She hated it when one set of plans got switched for another at the last minute. He could only imagine her feelings about changing centuries.

"Okay, hold it ... ," she put up a hand, "you've done

this *before*?"

"Yes, last Tuesday, when I was cleaning Grandma Geri's house. I found the sticks, lit one, and *whoosh*! American Revolution. Better than the History Channel. I waited a few days before I told anyone, and then I was *finally* able to get Roger alone and I told him about it and-"

"And you didn't tell me."

"Will you listen! I wanted to verify it with one person first, and then I was going to tell you about it. I didn't know if my first trip was just an illusion or what, so I asked Roger to sniff this one with me and see what happened. He agreed, and then, well, you walked in and the rest is history," he laughed, "so to speak."

Andy saw Miranda's wounded face. "This isn't personal, Miranda."

"I wanted to ask you to come down to the vet's with me, thought we could sign up to do some volunteering during the weekends," she explained.

"How could you know what was going on? It's not your fault."

She relented. "You're right. But now, we've got more important things to think about. How did you get back from wherever you were?"

"Boston, Miranda. It was unbelievable. It wasn't pretty. Those people," he paused. "There was so much hatred back then. All that anger and blood and..." Andy shuddered. "I got back by burning and sniffing the unused part of the incense stick I kept in my pocket. But what's really weird is when I returned, I was back to normal, wearing normal clothes and no time had passed. It was the same time as when I had left! No one had missed me. They didn't even know I was gone!"

"So, what are we doing here?" She stood up. "Let's go back! Good night, I've seen enough," she said as she picked up part of her lumbering dress and dropped it again, "and I've had enough of this!"

She froze and her face changed. "Oh! That's what you meant by what you said to Roger. We can't go back. You dropped the stick. It's on your bedroom floor."

"Bingo." He had been wracking his brain searching for an answer to their time travel troubles. "Sorry, I'm not being flip. It's just, we're stuck here, and I really don't know what we're going to do about that."

# Chapter Thirteen

Roger, after working all afternoon and keeping his mouth shut, knew a lot more information than Miranda and Andy. It was August, 1858, and he was Rufus. Just plain Rufus. And they were Miss Miriam and Master Drew. This was the state of Georgia. Roger filled in the gaps. The South would eventually secede from the North, and the Civil War was still four years away.

Rufus lived with five other people: his Aunt Rose and Uncle Steven, his younger brothers Leeks and Pete, and his cousin, Sweet Sue. Sweet Sue was pregnant, and her husband had been sold last month to a plantation in South Carolina. Rose did all of the cooking in the cabin since Sweet Sue was in the slave nursery/hospital waiting to give birth.

Sweet Sue, later, would die during childbearing, and her husband would never, ever see her again and never come to know his newborn child.

Of Rufus' parents, no one knew. Aunt Rose had last seen them six years ago at the slave auction. His mother was sold to an owner near Atlanta, and his father was shipped off to Mississippi. Rufus and his brothers were sold together with Rose, because the auctioneer thought that Rose was their mother instead of their aunt. He never bothered to check, or ask, nor did he really care.

The slave hospital, except for the Main House, was the cleanest building on the property. It was high off the ground, and anyone who was there was well fed and well tended. Strong, healthy baby slaves appreciated in value, so every expense was taken to make sure they were born that way. Pregnant slaves received extra clothing, food, and time off. They were excused from most of the work and even after they delivered a child, they were given minimal work so that they could tend to the feeding and caretaking of their newborns.

When the bell rang for the slaves to stop working and go back to their cabins, the group Roger was working with collectively sighed with relief.

"Another day," Aunt Rose said as they started walking toward the slave quarters.

Roger was absolutely exhausted. The muscles in his lower back ached, and his fingers and palms were stiff with pain. He looked at what direction the slaves were heading. Toward the right of the Main House. Toward these tiny buildings that only could be called "shacks;" buildings Roger had seen on PBS during documentaries on the Civil War.

*That can't be possible*, he thought as the people moved like unresponsive sheep toward their homes. *That can't be where we live.*

The slave cabins, unlike the hospital/nursery, were the most poorly constructed buildings on the site. Even the pigsty and the horse barn were better! The cabins were built of logs right on the ground. It would be like trying to camp with a tent that had no canvas floor. They were damp, and when it rained, the water seeped into the room. It rotted away the lowest timbers and created an environment where all kinds of molds and viruses could creep into the slaves' lungs. The logs were poorly put together, so Uncle Steven had put in large blotches of mud and straw to seal up the holes. The wooden shingles on the roof warped from the sun, and often the rain leaked from above. When it was cold, the wind blew through the cracks and made everyone miserable.

"This is incredible!" said Roger to himself when he arrived at his “home”. "We live in a sewer!"

The chimney wasn't built very securely, and often the smoke stayed in the room. Ventilation was awful and there was very little room inside. Roger staggered into the cabin and lay down on one of the thin, lumpy beds. His hands were blistered from the hoeing, and he felt depressed and hungry.

"Get up, Rufus!" Aunt Rose said as she started making supper. "Who do you think you are, King Solomon? Get some water for me, and then pull up some vegetables out of the garden. People are hungry!"

*It never ends*, thought Roger. *This is going to go on again tomorrow and the next day and the next.*

As he headed back outside again, at the doorway (it was just a rectangular hole in the wall, there was no actual door), wedged into the cracks of the wall, was a piece of paper. Roger pulled it out. It looked like a school note kids passed to each other in fourth grade. He unfolded it, and read:

MEET US TONIGHT IN THE HORSE BARN A HALF HOUR AFTER SUNSET.

It was signed, MIRANDA.

Uncle Steven came into the room with some more

chopped wood and grabbed the note out of Rufus' hand. "What's that?" he asked. "Where did you find this?"

"In the wall," said Roger.

"The *wall*! We are cursed! I knew it! Brandnew put a hex on this house 'cause her Marcy ain't pregnant and our Sweet Sue is!"

"No it's not," explained Roger. "It's a note from Miss Miriam. She wants me to -"

Steven grabbed Roger's arm and threw him against the far wall. He landed on the bed with an *ummph*.

"Don't you ever, *ever* say the words 'Miss Miriam,' do you hear me? Talking about a white girl like it's a game. You're fourteen! You want to see fifteen? Moxley'll string you up and pull that rope without a tear if you keep talking like that!" Uncle Steven's words crackled in the air as he headed toward Roger with a finger pointed at his nephew's head. The cabins were too close together without everyone hearing part of *some* conversation. He leaned down and grabbed Roger's face and squeezed. Roger felt the strong hand grab around his cheeks, and Uncle Steven pulled his face up toward him, toward the note.

"Your sister died because she thought she could out smart them. She couldn't. She drowned in the river trying to escape and you're no better. Remember that! A black boy talking about a white girl is a sure thing to a hanging."

He let loose on his nephew's face and stood up. "Go gather some vegetables for your aunt."

Uncle Steven took the paper and threw it into the

fire. "We undo your curse with the fire of prayer!"

Roger got up and went outside. Each cabin had a little patch of ground where every family could grow their own crops. Mostly, he remembered, slaves ate pork, corn meal, molasses, and sweet potatoes. Some turnips, some greens. Roger seemed to know which vegetables to pull up and which to leave in the ground. He was tugging at a carrot when he stopped short.

*They can't read*! he thought. *That's what triggered the anger. I forgot about that. But I can read, and they don't know that. No wonder Uncle Steven was thinking I was making a joke. Think Roger old boy... think! think! Don't slip up... and no more notes! For cripe's sake, I'll have to tell Miranda and Andy.*

MEET US TONIGHT IN THE HORSE BARN A HALF HOUR AFTER SUNSET.

Roger instinctively looked at his watch. He looked where his watch *should* have been. How am I supposed to know when it's a half hour? Roger hoped Andy had some plan to get them out of here because this was not fun. Never would be.

# CHAPTER FOURTEEN

When there are no streetlights or porch lights or even flashlights, the world, after sunset, is awfully dark. Roger, barely seeing the hand in front of his face, crept slowly and carefully out of his cabin. He wore no shoes and hoped that he wouldn't stub his toe on anything. The horse barn was close to the slave quarters.

*Of course. Heck, we're in the same category.*

He slinked toward the little creek that flowed through the property and almost fell down the small embankment. He avoided the tiny bridge and practically crawled down the bank to the stream. In three quick steps he was across the water, and he scrambled up the other side.

The horse barn was straight ahead of him. A shape loomed by the door. It pulled Roger inside. It was pitch black. Roger saw nothing, but felt the hand of his friend on his arm. Andy gave him a strong hug.

"Are you okay?" Andy said, "are you hungry?" He pushed a pear, or rather, what *smelled* like a pear into Roger's left hand.

"Andy," Roger whispered. "This isn't a dream, old friend. This is real. Whatever your Grandma Geri did, she acquired something very powerful. Those sticks are real, and this place is real, my blisters are real, my hunger is real." In four ravenous bites, the pear was gone. "My clothes, I'm sorry if I smell. I only have one pair of pants and 2 shirts. Gosh, I don't even have underwear!"

"Don't worry about that," Andy smiled. "Neither do I!"

Miranda flew into the barn door entrance and banged into both of them. "Don't *do that*!" she snarled.

"Sorry, we didn't hear you coming," offered Andy.

"I'm sorry I'm late, I didn't know what time it was. I couldn't see the clock in my room." Miranda was catching her breath. "It's so *dark* out here! Roger, this is awful. I can't see you, but are you all right? I mean, a slave! When I asked people which cabin was yours, everyone looked at me funny. I had to keep remembering where I was and what *color* I was."

"Miranda, I'm okay. Tired, and hungry, but I'm alive. We're in Georgia. It's 1858, it's August, and we're in the middle of harvest season. That much I know. I don't know where my parents are, but I have an aunt and uncle and two brothers who call me Rufus. My sister is dead."

While Roger was filling them in on what information he had discovered, Andy couldn't see him, but there was something in Roger's tone that made Andy take notice.

"Roger," said Andy.

Roger continued talking. "And there's Moxley, this overseer who-"

Andy interrupted, "Roger, I wish there was some way to take you off 'field duty' or whatever they call it."

"There's got to be," Roger said. "This is hell. You should see where I live: it's like we're rats or something. I've never worked so hard in my entire life. I keep thinking I'm going to wake up and this will be some god awful ancestral dream."

Miranda said, "When Andy was sleeping, I did a bunch of needlepoint today. *Needlepoint*! *Me*? I never did that in my life, but suddenly, in this world, I know how! Sort of like you knew how to suck out the poison, Roger."

Roger added, "It's as if these new, or rather, *old* identities we have are us! I mean, it *is* us, but we sort of inhabit these people who really lived once before! So, we know how to do everything they knew how to do."

"Miss Nancy wants me to give a piano recital tomorrow night," said Miranda, "and I'm not a bit nervous about it. I practiced my pieces this afternoon, and they sounded fine."

"You can't play the piano," said Andy.

Miranda laughed, "Back home, our family never *owned* a piano."

"Back home," Roger said, "our family never *owned* a slave."

Miranda stopped laughing.

Andy zeroed in on Roger, where Roger was standing. He couldn't see him, but he could feel Roger's vibrations emanating from him. He felt the anger brewing, bubbling.

"I've been thinking," Andy intervened. "Maybe the incense stick was an herb. I mean, it smelled like something I had smelled before. When I went to Boston, *that* stick sort of smelled like cranberries and turkey, you know, New England smells. But this stick was different. It smelled like," he struggled for a word, "I don't know ... something familiar."

"But so what, Andy? What's your point?" Roger snapped. "You dropped it! You dropped the only way we have of getting home."

"I have a feeling, just a gut feeling, that if we can identify the smell of the incense stick, say it is an herb or a flower or a vegetable or something, it might get us home." Andy felt Roger's anger rising and didn't know how to respond to it.

"You mean," asked Miranda, "all we have to do is find the vegetable, or whatever that smelled like that incense stick and wham! We zoom home? How? What are we supposed to do, *eat it*?"

"I don't know," said Andy, "maybe just burn it. Like when we burned the stick. Sniff the smoke and 'good-bye!'"

"Well I can just see me now, trying to burn a carrot or a sweet potato," said Roger. "Oh, and by the way, *no more notes*! My people weren't taught to read, remember? I almost was whipped because of that incident. I'm supposed to be illiterate. If you want to meet again, at night, leave me a sign."

"What if I draw an X in the dirt to the left of your cabin?" Andy asked. "When you come in at night, you can look for the signal. See the X and that means we meet in the horse barn a half hour after sunset."

*When you come in at night.*

Just like a cow.

Roger lost it.

"You stuck up *snob*!" he whispered with pure malice. "Do you have any idea what you put me through? You think this is some fantasy video game we're playing? *I'm a slave*! *A piece of property*! With just one word, you or Moxley can have me sold or chained up, even killed!"

Roger grabbed Andy by the front of his shirt. The pressure of his fist pulling on the shirt was so tight, Andy could hear it rip.

"I have to get up in the morning and *work*! I don't get a choice. Do you understand that? I don't get to decide to stay home and play baseball. I have to get up, before dawn, and work. Hard, grueling, hot, hot, hot work picking cotton! I overheard Moxley telling the foreman this afternoon. All of us have to get into the fields, excuse me, I mean all of us slaves have to get in the fields, bend over and *pick*!"

Andy felt Roger's fist getting stronger. Andy stood there, shell-shocked.

"What are *you two* going to be doing?" continued Roger. "Playing the piano? Learning some math?" In a twisted parody of a Southern accent he said, "Oh, Miriam, Ah'm so thirsty! Prissy, Mammie, whoever you are, get me a cool drink of water!"

Roger spat on the ground and spat out the words. "I'm going to be out there every ... single ... day Andy Mackpeace, and *you had better come up with something better than let's play 'find the freakin vegetable*'!!"

Roger pushed Andy so hard, the boy fell down, and since it was completely dark, no one knew if Andy landed on some hay or a pitchfork.

"Okay, now hold it!" Miranda commanded. "Stop. Just stop." She reached out her palm to put it on Roger. In the darkness, it magically found its mark and her hand landed on his chest, right where his heart was. It was beating rapidly.

"Stop," she said again. "Stop that thinking. We are in this together. We. Are. In. This. Together. There is no 'they.'"

Andy came back to his feet.

"I remember the smell of the incense stick," Miranda went on, "and I bet you do too, Roger. Andy may have a point. Find something, heck, *anything* that matches that smell, and it may, it just may get us home. If we can burn it, then *maybe*, when we sniff it, we are free. *All of us. Free.*"

Roger's heart slowed down. His breathing steadied.

"Roger," Andy said. "I know you're angry, I know this is unbelievable. I wish I could change the time, I wish I could change everything, but I can't."

"I'm sorry I pushed you, Andy," Roger said. "That was pretty childish. I just don't know what to do. I feel absolutely powerless. But hey, maybe Miranda's right. Finding anything remotely similar is worth a try. It's at least *something* to go on."

This time it was Roger who reached for Andy and gave him a hug. "I'm sorry goes to you too, Miranda. I won't be able to do too much investigating tomorrow, but I'll sniff every plant and piece of food I get my hands on. It might be as simple as all those cotton plants I'll be facing!"

"Let's hope it's that simple," said Andy. "We could

be home by noon."

The three friends didn't realize that it really wasn't that simple, and when the next day came, none of them were home by noon.

# Chapter Fifteen

Day after day, the routine never changed. Roger rose every morning at 5:30, washed, ate and worked. At noon, house slaves brought food out to the cotton fields, and everyone ate it under the cool pine trees. At 2:00, if he hadn't passed out from the heat, Roger and the other slaves were given a two-hour break. They slept in the shade and drank water. The large bell hanging on the rafter in the yard near the Main House was struck every time there was a change in the routine. A bell to begin work, a bell to stop and eat, a bell at 4:00 to rouse everyone back into the fields. At 8:30, the last bell clanged and the field slaves trooped back to their homes.

Roger sometimes came home to secret food wrapped and stored under his bed. Although Andy couldn't get Roger off of "field duty," usually Andy was able to steal some large pieces of chicken or ham and stow it in his cabin. He'd wrap up some extra vegetables and fruit as well, anything that could help his friend survive. Uncle Steven knew Roger was somehow connected to this mysterious blessing, but because it was food for the family, and they were always hungry, he didn't question the boy. Roger had told him it was from one of the Main House slaves who sort of liked him and left it at that.

"As long as no one gets caught," said Uncle Steven. "If that happens, you're on your own!"

Miranda had the freedom to roam about the plantation, but never off the property alone. That would have been unseemly to go traipsing about without an escort. She, too, tried to relocate Roger to the Main house, but her mother shook her head.

"He's better off in the fields," she told her. "He's too strong for normal house work."

Miranda was not allowed to go near the slave quarters at all. After she put the note into Roger's wall, her father severely yelled at her.

"*Never* go in there again, Miriam," Mr. Finlayson admonished. "They are full of lice and disease!" So she wore those heavy dresses and her uncomfortable bonnet and poked in the kitchen as often as possible.

"What are you looking *for*, Miss Miriam?" Petunia asked that afternoon. Petunia was not much older than Miranda. She was the main cook's helper, and she was also in charge of the herb garden. "Are you hungry?"

Petunia really couldn't prevent Miranda from wandering through the kitchen and the gardens; Miss Miriam had never peered around like that before. Miranda wandered out of the kitchen, through the vegetable garden and was standing among the herbs.

"I'm hoping to learn all about these, Petunia," Miranda said. "I want to follow in Mama's footsteps on being the plantation doctor." Petunia was weeding some of the herbs nearby; the sun looked about three in the afternoon, and the garden was slightly shaded. It was cool enough for Miranda to linger awhile. She watched Petunia as she bent over each plant, half talking to them and pulling out weeds. "Do you know about the medicines of these herbs, Petunia?"

"Most," she said. "My mama used to know all of these; I think that's why they made me in charge of this after she left." Petunia stopped weeding for a moment and stood up. She was slender, healthy. The house slaves usually were healthier: they had better food to eat. Petunia was strong and determined. Miranda thought she looked rather like a very capable field hockey player she would want on her team.

In five years, in 1863 when the Emancipation Proclamation was finally authorized, Petunia would leave Glendower Plantation for good. She would be 21 years old. She would walk all the way to Savannah and steal on board a ship going to the Bahamas. At Nassau she would stay, living happily in a town where she would be respected as the medicine woman. Her knowledge of herbs and remedies would bring many people to her door, for her wisdom would go far beyond the medicines of the time. She would die in 1924 a peaceful death, fitting of such a peace- filled woman.

"Where did your mama go?" asked Miranda. She walked slowly towards Petunia, minding the delicate herbs beneath her. "Was she sold off?"

"Happened almost nine years ago. You were a child at the time. You wouldn't have remembered her. It was February." Petunia had never told this story out loud before. "I was seven years old and had been playing with the other children near the slave cemetery. It was a cold day, and the cemetery is a damp place to be playing. We were daring each other to run and touch the gravestones. When I came home, I had already started coughing. Two days later and still coughing, my mother began making her medicines. She made the plasters and laid them on my chest. I drank the redroot tea and stayed inside all day."

Petunia stopped talking and looked into the trees. A minute later she started weeding again.

"So what happened?"

Petunia hesitated, took a deep breath, and continued. "My coughing got worse; it was the pneumonia. I was coughing and throwing up so much, I couldn't keep anything down. Every night, my mama would lie with me, hold onto me and keep me from shivering. It was like she was keeping me alive, just by holding me. I got weaker and weaker, but my mama kept giving me the plasters and staying with me."

Petunia stopped her fussing with the plants and turned toward Miranda.

"All of a sudden, one morning, I woke up and I started to get better. And the moment I started to feel better, my mama started to feel worse." She shook her head at the irony. "It was like she had been sucking the pneumonia right out of me, and taking it on herself. The only way her little girl was going to live is if she took it away herself. So she did. Night after night she wrapped her arms around me while I slept and she breathed in all that sickness. Pretty soon, my mama was too weak to get out of bed. I wanted to hold her, like she had held me, but she yelled at me whenever I got too close to her. She didn't want me to get sick all over again. Miss Nancy came and tried to help, but nothing worked. I sat in the room one night, there with

Miss Nancy. My mama had her eyes closed and was breathing really hard. It was like she was drowning. She opened her eyes and looked at me. 'Don't cry Petunia,' she said, 'your mama's right here.' She closed her eyes again, 'always will be.' My mama was gone. They buried her by the willow tree, a very pretty spot, Miss Nancy made sure of that."

"I don't remember much about my mama," added Petunia. "I don't remember what she looked like, but every once in a while I remember the smell of her dress. Isn't that strange?"

Miranda stood very still. Two tiny tears crept into the corner of her eyes, and she felt them slide down her face. "Oh Petunia," she wanted to say. "I'm from another time and place. They have cures for pneumonia now." But she didn't, and she knew that even if she could go over and hug Petunia, it would be seen as odd and might get Petunia in trouble.

"I'm sorry, Petunia," she said.

Petunia looked at this lovely white child, and Miranda looked right back, and together they stood in the middle of that herb garden, waiting for a time when all barriers would be broken.

# Chapter Sixteen

Andy's time travel father, Mr. Finlayson forced him to stay nearby and learn the ways of plantation operations. Andy had to sit in on meetings with his father and Moxley and look at accounting books and financial records. He learned about the planting of the various crops, and his father handed him agriculture manuals to read and memorize. He inspected all the livestock, the rise and fall of market prices, and the value of slave maintenance.

"If your slaves start dying on ya, you're in big trouble!" Moxley said. "You have to keep an eye out for runaways and sickness. If a slave ain't happy, he gets sick."

*Great advice*, thought Andy trying not to roll his eyes. *Gee, I wonder why there are twelve people in the slave hospital with pneumonia and cholera.* "Why don't we give them more food?" Andy offered. "More food means healthier bodies which mean less sickness! Plus, why are their cabins so damp!? Wouldn't it be better to give them-"

"Keep giving, and you'll have nothing left," snapped Moxley. "Those people have to be kept down. They have to know who's in charge. You start giving 'em things, and they'll start easing up on you. Pretty soon you'll find them sleeping in the fields from all the food in their stomachs. Hunger gives them the drive! If they don't work, they don't eat. Rule of the plantation."

Andy just looked at him.

Moxley hacked his throat, turned his head, and spat into the yard as if talking about them had become some vile slave taste in his mouth.

Although Moxley's hatred of the slaves was checked regularly by Mr. Finlayson, often the owner stepped back when true disciplining had to be done. Moxley's authority had to be established and respected, and if it meant an occasional whipping or slapping a lazy slave or extra hours at work, then so be it. If one of them died in the course of running away, well, he or she deserved it. In 1858, people like Moxley and Mr. Finlayson thought slaves were half animals. Give them some food and a place out of the rain in which to sleep, and they were fine. Work 'em til they drop.

Later that afternoon, when there was a brief respite from the work, Andy found Miranda in the blueberry bushes at the top of the hill behind the Main House. She was looking for the special incense smell. She sniffed the berries, the leaves, the branches and was down on her knees sniffing the roots when he told her about that horror called Moxley.

"Good Lord, Miriam! What are you doing?" Mrs. Finlayson yelled up to them from the bottom of the hill. "Are you sick?"

"I guess saying, 'I lost my contact lens' wouldn't exactly be appropriate right now," said Miranda to Andy. "I saw a baby rabbit!" she yelled back.

The trouble was there were literally hundreds of plants and vegetables on the site. They were drying, growing, blossoming, dying, or being harvested. All afternoon, for four hours, Andy and Miranda searched everywhere and sniffed everything. The herb garden alone contained seventy-eight different herbs, and not all of them were growing at the same time.

"What if what we're supposed to smell isn't ripe yet or already bloomed last month?" asked Miranda. "We could be stuck here until next spring!"

"Well, that gets us off the hook with eighth grade. We can just skip it altogether!"

"I've been smelling everything in the food, have you? That venison we had last night was -"

"That was venison!" interrupted Andy. "Good night, I thought it was some weird kind of beef! We were eating Bambi?"

"Get a grip," said Miranda, who was pulling up some arugula and sniffing the leaves. "We're in the 19th century! What do you think we were eating? My point is I sniff everything, even in something like that. The incense stick," she shook her head, "I can't find words to describe what it smelled like, but I do know that I'll recognize it when I smell it!"

"This could take forever," Andy said.

He wandered through the herb garden and starting kicking the leaves of the plants, hoping for that smell to waft up into his nostrils. There was sage, thyme, rosemary, peppermints and spearmints and lemony smelling mints. The smells accosted him and blended and started to make his head ache.

"I don't even know what half of these plants are called," he whined.

"In one way, it doesn't matter what they're called. Just keep looking for that smell." Miranda stood up again. "I've been thinking, maybe the smell is a combination of things, or something you have in a tea. You know like those teas we used to drink: 'Sleepy Tea' or 'Relax' They were a blend of different herbs, like chamomile, lemongrass and licorice, remember?"

"Good grief, Miranda, if it's a combo menu we're looking for, we could be here until we die," argued Andy.

His boot hit one particular lavender branch, hard and tangling and he almost tripped. He yanked it up by its roots and threw it as hard as he could at the kitchen wall.

"Crap!" he yelled. It was very hot by late afternoon, and Andy was frustrated and irritated. Grandma Geri used to chide him on his irritability.

"It does no good to anyone to be miserable and ornery," she'd say. "It serves no purpose to life. The answers will come when they're supposed to." She would swirl her arms in a sorceress sort of way. "Stop trying to make it happen! It will come to you."

"But what about *now*, Grandma, what do we do about now?" Andy said aloud.

"What did you say?" asked Miranda. "Did you find something useful?"

"Just talking to my grandmother," said Andy growing a little red.

"What's she saying?" said Miranda, who loved the idea of talking to dead grandmothers. "Any leads?"

"She told me, well, I *guess* she told me, she used to tell me in the *past* anyway, whenever I felt frustrated, to stop trying to force things to happen. Relax into it, and the answers will appear. *It* will come to us."

Miranda started twirling in all directions, looking north, south, east, and west. "I'm looking for any vegetables heading my way!" she said.

She stopped and looked at her beloved friend. He started to laugh and she joined him. Two misplaced time travelers on far ends of a giant herb garden.

"Yes," said Andy. "We're in this together. All three of us."

The large black bell rang from the rafter. The sound pealed out into the cotton fields, and the barn, and the slave quarters, and the creek, and the roads and trees beyond. It rang on into the century and told of a life that would no longer exist.

"Supper time, Master Drew!" said Petunia, "What are you two doing standing in the middle of my herb garden?"

"Coming, Petunia," said Miranda, sweating and muttering under her breath. "This dress is going to make me lose my mind."

# Chapter Seventeen

The full moon awoke Andy at a quarter to one. The light streamed through his window and onto his face, much like the street lamp outside his home used to. The Main House was ghoulishly quiet. No hum of a refrigerator or microwave or a computer monitor. No dishwasher running or dryer tumbling. Electronic sounds that would sometimes jar him awake back home now were completely absent. He slid off the poster bed and walked in his bare feet toward the open window. The moon made the plantation look blue: as if it had snowed. The smells of the horses floated by, he heard the trickle of the stream and the sound of an owl. Cicadas. Other than that, there was nothing. There were a few stars on the farther side of the sky, but the moonlight reminded him of summer nights at home.

*It's the same moon*, he thought. *It shone on them as it shines on us.*

It had been six days. Six days with no new discoveries.

Andy figured that someone at home by now has got to have missed him. When he traveled back to Boston, his trip was brief and the present time hadn't been affected.

But what about after six days?

Andy didn't have an answer for that. How long does time stop before it starts to pick up again? He could picture his father coming into his bedroom and seeing the opened door and the little pile of matches and the incense stick. His father would think he'd been smoking dope or cigarettes, and he'd be walking around talking to his mom. "I didn't think we'd have to worry about this with our Andy," he could hear his father say.

Worse yet! What if his father came into his room, saw the incense, and then lit one! He could end up here! Well, that would be fine as long as he had some extra in his pocket!

*Oh Grandma*, Andy thought as he gazed out over the beautiful land and smelled the sweet, country air. *How are we going to get out of here? What's this all about*?

Sometimes, in the summer, or on a crisp, windless winter night, Andy and Grandma Geri went out into the back fields and stargazed. Grandma Geri had a small telescope, and she taught him the names of constellations and the brighter stars.

"See *that* one?" she said one time, pointing to a gorgeous red star in the Southern sky. It was the middle of August when Andy was about ten years old. "That's Antares, one of my favorite. It's in the constellation Scorpio; you can see that it looks like a Scorpion. With a flashlight, she traced in the sky, from star to star, a giant "J" swerving off to the left. There, about halfway down, was Antares. "Antares is six-hundred light years away from Earth."

"It'd take six-hundred years to get there?" Andy asked. How could he see that red star so clearly when it was so far away?

"Well, sort of. First, you'd have to be traveling the speed of light, which is 186,300 miles *per second*. Per second, Andy! Can you imagine whirling through space that quickly?" She took the flashlight and swooshed it across the night sky like a meteor. "Then, if you're really going that fast, it would take you six-hundred years to get there. And who knows what planets would be waiting for you when you arrived?"

"I can't imagine that far," said Andy.

"I can't either, honey," she said, "but it's a wonderful feeling trying. Oh, the things out there!" She put her arms around his shoulders and together they surveyed the heavens. The night was full of the sounds of crickets and frogs. "There are galaxies, and moons, and planets, and billions and billions of stars. We're so tiny sitting here," she breathed in the hay and the fresh air, "but how precious and magical that is."

Andy sat on the windowsill in the moonlit, timeless, plantation house. The sounds of the night swirled around him, and the minutes of the hour traveled onward. He was Andy and he was Drew.

After a moment, he caught himself dozing off, and he jerked his head awake. A shooting star caught his eye. Andy felt completely connected to all that he saw. It was the most peaceful feeling he ever had, and as Andy breathed, the universe breathed.

He was now and he was then. The trees are planted and people are born; the trees are cut down and people die. It could be the 21st Century, it could be the 19th. "The time doesn't matter, Andy," he heard Grandma Geri say. "We're in the rhythm of the stars and the tunes of the planets, and always shall be."

# Chapter Eighteen

The next morning, Roger was finishing the last bit of his pathetic breakfast, and was heading out with Uncle Steven and Aunt Rose toward the direction of the fields. His back ached, and his right hand was cramped from all the picking. His feet had cracked badly two days ago, but Aunt Rose rubbed a little pork fat on them every night to heal the soreness. Roger was becoming numb to work.

Day after day, the same, tedious awful work was wearing him down. Despite the pain in his fingers and toes, he was in good health, but mentally, he was beaten. His determination for finding a way out of there was gone. He couldn't think beyond the next cotton plant. Freedom became a light that grew dimmer and dimmer until he believed he would never leave this place.

His family persevered, and for their sanity and health, Roger too persevered. He vowed not to let them down or make them feel ashamed of him. So, he got up like the rest of the slaves, ate the meager meal, worked, and didn't complain.

Sometimes, in the afternoon heat, he passed out from exhaustion, but so did some of the other people his age. When it happened, one of the men carried him into the shade and later, when he woke up, an older woman handed him a cup of water. He was excused from working for an hour, but when it turned a bit cooler, he was forced to resume the picking. Harvest was the busiest time and no one was deserved of special treatment. If you could stand, you could pick.

Uncle Steven spent much time with Roger and taught him about the earth, about the ground. He taught him the way a plant grows and how to read the sky for signs of a weather change. He pointed out different birds and taught him their birdcalls. He showed Roger how to talk with the animals and understand their ways. For Roger, this all seemed unusually familiar. It was sort of hidden, or buried within him, like relearning last year's math on the first day of school.

Yesterday afternoon, the slaves in Roger's section of the field started singing. Moxley, drinking water in the shade, sat on his horse overlooking the work force and smiled. "Singing slaves are happy slaves!" he said to the foreman.

Roger instinctively knew that nothing could be further from the truth. The rhythm, the underlying hum of the songs said, "We are a people in bondage. We are miserable. We are a people with history and you are one of us." The songs vibrated into the earth, into the soil.

Roger remembered in fifth grade what his music teacher Mr. Woodrow had taught them: "Slave songs were freedom songs. They used the words of the song as a code to pass on information about how to become free, how to persevere."

Roger learned the words and sang with the others. He connected to his people and the hidden language that was their only weapon against this horrible situation. The songs were the key that unlocked their prisons. Each of them knew that. Silently, they knew that.

A bit of morning sunshine broke Roger's thoughts.

"Rufus, take your two brothers over to the Child House and then meet us in the corn field. We're picking corn today, for a change," Aunt Rose said while she was putting on her shoes and getting Leeks and Pete ready at the same time.

The Child House was the babysitting house for the child slaves too young to work in the fields. The older slave women watched and cared for the children all day. Some of the children had orders to haul wood or feed the farm animals. Some of them had to help clean the stalls or wash the clothes. When not working, they were allowed to play.

Roger stretched his body, took his two brothers, and was about to step outside, when Moxley stood in the doorway.

"You lyin', sneakin' thief!" he said while each word got louder and louder. He grabbed Roger by the back of his neck and threw him outside into the dirt.

* * *

"Another hot day," Miranda grumbled as she bumbled her way to breakfast. "Doesn't it rain?"

Andy was already seated when she walked into the pristine dining room. The china was glistening and the sideboard was filled with covered dishes of eggs and bacon and breads and potatoes. Their father too was seated and was spasmodically coughing. It was a persistent cough, full of phlegm which Mr. Finlayson spat out into a small bowl placed discretely near his boots.

Miranda turned a bit green and focused on her eggs. They were runny and undercooked and she soaked up some of it with a piece of bread. As she was about to pop it into her mouth, her father popped a large one into the bowl. She turned greener, gritted her teeth and ate the bread, yolk and all.

Andy was finishing the last of his toast when the master's personal house slave, James, came into the dining room carrying a pot of tea. He placed it in front of Mr. Finlayson, nodded his head, and left.

"Finally!" said Miss Nancy. "I told Petunia to brew it earlier this morning! Now that," she pointed at the pot, "will clear up that coughing! You and your lung problems, John, you have to stay away from the slave quarters. Let Moxley go in there."

Andy and Miranda froze. The tea. ***THE SMELL***! It was THE SMELL! The incense smell! They looked at each other in utter disbelief. *There it was*! That lovely, gorgeous, sweet, yet earthy, this-will-get-us-home *smell*! "Mama," said Miranda, "please, what kind of tea is that? It smells heavenly."

"It's for your father's lungs," her mother said. "It's the perfect cure for cleaning out the fluids. It's called-"

A horrendous scream broke through the house.

"*No, please Mr. Moxley*!! Don't!" Aunt Rose yelled with all her might so Mr. Finlayson might come out and stop this awful assault on her nephew Rufus. She screamed again, even louder.

Everyone raced out of the dining room and ran down the stairs to the back door. Everyone, except

Andy and Miranda. They jumped up, like their family, but they hadn't moved and no one noticed them. They went over to the tea. It was still in the pot, steaming, brewing. They leaned over and smelled it.

"It's it! Isn't it?" asked Andy. "It's the same smell as what we smelled, right?"

"Yes!" Miranda stared at the cup as if it were trying to tell her something. "It definitely is. It's here. It's from something grown. Something that is brewable. Andy, we can go home!"

She reached across to her place setting and grabbed her little china cup. As if approaching a bottle that contained a genie, she picked up the teapot and poured some into the cup. It smelled even stronger.

"Master Drew, the master wants you!" James popped in his head and waited for him. "It is very important!"

That kind of command from his father could not be ignored.

"Drink it, Miranda, drink it!" Andy whispered. "Go home, get the stick, and come back. It'll take you right here. I know it. Then find me!"

Miranda hesitated. *I can't leave you behind*, her look said.

"Do it!" Andy insisted. He left her standing there and followed James out of the room.

Miranda stared at the brew and then lifted the cup to her mouth. It was hot, but with one determined grimace, she placed the liquid to her mouth, closed her eyes, and swallowed.

# Chapter Nineteen

Nothing happened.

Miranda opened her eyes and saw the sunlight coming through the window, the cold breakfast sitting on plates, even her father's phlegm bowl.

"Damn!" she said. "It doesn't work this way!"

She stood by a chair, holding that ridiculous cup, thinking and thinking. She was jarred back to reality by another scream from Aunt Rose.

"What is going on out there?" she said aloud as she headed out of the dining room, down the stairs, and toward the back door. She opened the door and saw a horrible commotion happening near the slave quarters. People were standing in a circle, and Moxley and Roger were in the middle.

"Stop, please Mr. Moxley, please stop!" Aunt Rose pleaded.

Moxley was picking Roger up and throwing him back down in the dirt again. As he grabbed Roger and hauled him to his feet, Mr. Finlayson and Andy stepped into the circle.

Moxley instantly stopped.

"This is the one who's been stealing our food," Moxley said. "I could smell the chicken as I was making the rounds this morning." He turned on Roger. "You're just like your sister, aren't ya? You think you're so smart you can steal our food and think no one notices! I'm going to teach you not to steal again!" He pushed Roger again into the dirt and was about to kick him.

"All right, Mr. Moxley, that's enough," Andy's father said in a very strange, calm voice. The plantation owner's word was law, and Moxley stopped his kick in mid air.

"Is it true you've been stealing, Rufus?" Mr. Finlayson asked.

Roger stood up. There was dirt in his mouth, and the dust stung in his eyes. He wiped them once. He looked at Uncle Steven and Aunt Rose. His relatives were stone faced. His eyes told them that he knew he was in a predicament that could have his entire family sold off, beaten, or worse yet, killed. Roger then turned to look at Mr. Finlayson. He saw the patient look in the man's eye as he waited for his answer.

Andy wanted to intercede. Andy thought that if he spoke up and told the truth, how it was he who had stolen the food, Roger would not be punished.

*It's just some ham, parts of a chicken*, Andy thought. *It's not like it's a bank or a jewelry store.*

From Andy's point of view, an embarrassed confession would leave everyone laughing. Roger knew otherwise.

*You don't get it, do you*? Andy felt Roger's eyes talking to him. *Despite all of your straight A's in school, you don't understand. It's not that simple, Andy.*

Just as Andy was about to open his mouth to speak, Roger spoke even louder. "Yes, sir. At night. I was hungry sir."

"Thank you, Rufus."

Mr. Finlayson was so calm. He nodded his head once and seemed about to walk away. Andy sighed with relief and smiled. It was over, and Roger would be fine.

"Get the whip, Mr. Moxley," Andy's father continued. "Rufus, stand over by that tree and take off your shirt. Mr. Moxley, you're too strong for this. He's just a boy; have Drew do it."

With that announcement, he walked away, back to his breakfast, back to his tea.

# Chapter Twenty

At Glendower, slave whippings were used to break down resistance, to break down any aggressions. Mr. Finlayson or Moxley used a whip that was three and a half feet long made out of cowhide. On the tip of it was the "cracker": twelve inches of soft buckskin "fingers" that would sting the slave. Only the cracker was supposed to touch the slave's back: it stung horribly, but did not break the skin. While other plantation owners took great pleasure in inflicting blood-producing gashes on their slaves to show them their cruel power, not Mr. Finlayson, not at Glendower. John Finlayson wanted to keep his property in good physical condition. Thirty lashes of deep, openly festering sores left him with one less slave for the fields, and harvesting time was not the time for that!

With Mr. Finlayson, there was no discussion, no pleading for mercy. His word was law. The whippings hurt the slave, yes, but the terrible punishment did much more than simply sting. It broke the human spirit down: it humiliated a human being in front of his family and his other workers. Mr. Finlayson's rule on the plantation during a whipping was that every slave, house or field, had to watch the punishment. It was as if to say, "See that? That could happen to you."

All the slaves gathered and stood in a circle, watching, praying. Andy watched Moxley head toward the barn. He crossed over the bridge and ducked into the building briefly and returned carrying the *thing* in his left hand. Mr. Finlayson, by now, was back in the dining room, drinking his tea and thinking of other things.

Moxley, with a crooked smile on his face, sauntered over to Andy. Andy looked at him and started shaking his head.

"Okay, Drew," he said, "here ya go, son. It's just like you practiced, on the watermelon, remember? Give him fifteen lashes for starters."

"You can't do that!" Miranda shouted. "It's -"

"Go inside the house if you don't want to watch, Miss Miriam," barked Moxley.

"I'm not moving!" she barked back. At the sound of her voice Andy snapped his head in her direction. She made an 'it didn't work' face.

"Go inside," her mother said. "This isn't for you."

"I'm not going anywhere!" Miranda gripped the railing and watched the scene below her.

Moxley put the whip into Andy's hands and pushed him over to Roger. Roger was standing facing a tree, a tall, solid looking tree just on the edge of the slave cabins. When he heard the two of them approaching, Roger turned his head and tried to speak. But his face was frozen. “Don't do this,” his look said. “Don't do this to me.”

Andy was about four feet away from Roger and felt all the slaves' eyes on him. The whip felt coarse and evil. It had been used before, he was sure of it.

"You'll be owner of this place someday, Drew," Moxley whispered into his ear with a lecherous snarl. "Now *show* them."

"No," Andy whispered. "I can't. Please, I can't hit

another person. He did nothing wrong. I can't ... " Andy's knees buckled a bit and he started to keel over, but Moxley grabbed his arm and pulled him up.

"Do it!" he said. His eyes were piercing Andy's skull and he shook Andy with determination. "You're the boss now! Walk away, and you're not a man. Walk away, and your father will never forgive you. He'll punish you a lot worse than that boy."

Moxley gripped Andy like an iron clamp. With every word he uttered, Moxley's spit hit Andy's face and his stomach turned over.

Andy and Roger stared at each other. No chasm in the world could have been wider. Andy raced through his brain trying to find some logical sense, some way out of this situation.

Moxley swore. "Turn around you!" he yelled at Roger. "Look at that tree! Turn around again, and *I'll* do the whipping!"

Roger turned around and instinctively knew to raise his arms and lean against the trunk. His face was three inches from the bark. He smelled the texture of the tree. Andy, defeated, lifted the whip and started twirling it in a circle above his head.

"Stop!" Miranda said, coming down the stairs.

"You take one more step, girl," Miss Nancy's voice cracked like ice. "And I'll give you a whipping you won't ever forget."

Miranda's foot ended in mid-air.

"That's it boy. Get it going really fast!" the vile overseer said.

The whip whistled slightly and started to take on an

energy of its own. Andy kept control of it and kept his eyes on Roger's back. His stomach was churning and churning and he did everything he could do to keep his breakfast down. Andy twirled the whip, around and around.

Roger heard the *whing, whing* of the whip, tightened up his back muscles, and prepared for the hit.

*I'm sorry, Roger*, Andy thought, and he snapped it outward.

Roger screamed.

It was as if a giant bee had stung him across his back. A bee that stung him several times at once in a crossways motion from right to left.

Andy jumped at the noise. He let the whip lash to the ground. "I can't, Mr. Moxley," he said. "Please don't make me. I promise, I'll -"

"Shut up!" Moxley roared. "What kind of lousy, pathetic weakling are you? Do it, or I'll do it! Do it, or I'll take you down to the river where the snakes are!"

Andy picked the whip up off the ground. He started swirling it over his head then let it fly.

The whip slashed against Roger's raw skin, a slap sound that made everyone shudder as Roger's scream cut through the air.

Aunt Rose shut her eyes. *Just like his sister*, she said silently. Again.

"Please," she prayed, "let it be over soon."

Again.

Each time, Roger yelled out. Every assault stung worse than the one before. The pain became unbearable.

Miranda's eyes went from the whip to Andy to the whip to Roger.

Again.

"Stop," she said to herself. "Andy, stop. Stop it."

Again.

Roger's legs collapsed beneath him, and as he grabbed the bark to stay standing, he slid down to his knees. The bark cut into his palms which started bleeding; it was nothing compared to the pains on his back.

No matter if Roger was standing or kneeling, Andy hit him squarely on the back every time. Moxley was counting out loud next to him.

"Six," the overseer said. "Hit him!"

Andy felt cut in two. It was the spirit of the original Drew who was in control, making decisions based on a life and time he firmly believed. Whipping was justice and it had to be done. Andy's power, his voice, was completely gone.

"Seven!" Moxley cheered. "You won't ever steal again!"

"Eight."

"Nine! You'll keep your hands off our food now!" Moxley yelled.

"Ten."

"*Andy*!" Miranda screamed, her voice blasting through time shattering Andy out of his trance. "This is *not* justice," she said. "This is *not* who you are!"

Andy landed hard into his new reality. It was as she had slapped him across the side of his head. He turned to Miranda and her pleading face. He opened and closed his eyes as he adjusted to his new perception.

The slaves came back into view, Miss Nancy, Roger kneeling against the tree, stoic, not moving, Moxley's sour breath counting in his ear, that annoying, foul stench of the overseer that was in his face.

His rage erupted.

"*That's it*! No more!" Andy yelled, pushing the overseer out of his way.

"Your father wants fifteen, son, that's the rule."

"*Well, I'm not doing fifteen*!!" He turned and hurled the whip, flinging it far out of sight, where it tumbled down the embankment and fell into the stream.

There was complete silence.

Andy stood planted on the ground, but there were tears in his eyes. His mouth was quivering. "I'm not going to cry," he willed himself. "I am *not* in the fourth grade, and I don't want *anyone* to rescue me!" He wiped his eyes with his fist.

He kept his voice firm and loud. "If he wants to punish me, then let him punish me, but this *show*, Moxley, is over! Rufus, put your shirt on. Rose, tend to your nephew. The rest of you," Andy looked around at all the astonished faces, "get into the fields, and Moxley, get on your horse and go do your job."

Andy stormed across the bridge in the direction of the Main House. He avoided the plantation and walked around it into the orchard. The smells of the different fruit trees surrounded him and he stumbled into the dark grove and dove into the dirt.

He raised his right arm and pounded the uneven ground and roots. Again and again he slammed his fist and smashed some of the rotten pears and plums lying around him. He hit them so hard that they burst on impact and splattered into his face and his hair.

"You idiot!" he yelled at himself as he hit the earth. "You animal, you stupid piece of -" Every swear word he could think of came pouring out of his mouth. His right hand hurt and began to bruise. He didn't care.

Andy curled up into a ball and cried.

"I'm sorry, Roger," he said. He rocked back and forth feeling the roots of an apple tree dig into his back while trying to alleviate the gnawing, churning hopelessness in his belly.

"I'm sorry, Roger," he mumbled. "I'm sorry. I'm sorry."

"He knows that."

It was Miranda. She had followed him, and in his anger and disgust at himself, Andy never heard her enter the shadowy orchard.

"Go away," Andy moaned keeping his head buried. "I'm a coward, a weak, pathetic idiot who betrayed a friend rather than stand up to that stupid Moxley."

Andy's loud moans and whimpers traveled toward the open plantation windows.

"Shhh, don't let them hear you."

"I don't care who hears me! What difference does it make? Will you please go away and leave me alone!"

Miranda had no intention of going away. "Andy, this time travel, we're not immune from it. None of us are above the consequences of living in 1858."

"I *beat* him, Miranda, I beat my best friend. How could I do that? What made me do *that*?"

Andy couldn't stop the pain any longer. He leaned

over and threw up. Pieces of toast and chunks of oatmeal splattered on the roots and the rocks and ricocheted onto Miranda's dress and shoes. She ignored this and held onto his shoulders, then gave him her handkerchief. He paused for a minute, started to wipe the vomit from his nose when the second wave hit. He turned away from her just as another round of breakfast hit the side of the tree.

Andy crawled away from the smelly mess and collapsed on his side in the grass. He kept his eyes closed. He heard Miranda follow him.

"I'm no good," he said and gobbed up some bile. "I'm everything I was taught not to be."

She touched his bent knee with the palm of her hand while Andy's breathing slowed down.

"Focus on the breathing, Andy."

Andy's stomach settled down, stopped its churning. For a surprised minute, he fell asleep and when he came to, he sensed the soft shadows of the plantation cool in the damp grass. He heard the birds chirping, smelled the fruit trees.

He opened his eyes. Nothing had changed. The guilt hadn't gone. Now, it lived with him.

"Oh God, we're still here," he said.

"You're fuzzy," she said. "Take your time getting up."

He nodded toward the dining room window.

"The tea didn't do a thing except burn the roof of my mouth," Miranda answered. "My guess is whatever herb made that tea has to be ignited, then sniffed."

"We can do it, Miranda. If there's one thing I can do

to redeem myself, it's to find that blasted herb and get us out of here." He felt a new energy pulsing through him. "We'll find it today, and I'll leave an X for Roger. We'll meet in the barn tonight, light that thing, and go home."

Andy sighed, thinking about the ruined friendship, the impossibility of forgiveness. "Roger'll never talk to me again, but at least, we'll be home."

Miranda took Andy's arm and pulled him to his feet.

"I know exactly where to start," she said, and they went to find Petunia.

# Chapter Twenty-One

Petunia was weeding in her precious herb garden. Petunia had seen many whippings in her short lifetime, and she had seen two lynchings at Glendower.

The tone of the slaves changed after any punishment. Any sense of happiness or laughter or optimism vanished. They would, once again, painfully understand the simple truth: they were property. They were hated. If anyone didn't follow the rules, she was punished.

Petunia remembered the husband and wife who were lynched. They were young and very, very angry. They had plotted and schemed to run away. They worked as little as possible and refused to learn any English. They spoke in a language no one else understood and that made the master extremely nervous. After their third attempt at escaping the plantation, Mr. Finlayson, yelled, "Enough with this nonsense. Get some rope, Moxley!"

The slaves had to stand by and watch, Petunia recalled. Watch as two human beings were hanged in a tree. Afterward, Petunia helped some of the women prepare the bodies for burial. She washed the dead woman and dressed her and hoped she was happy now.

Petunia started picking some fresh herbs. The sun was not as strong today, there were clouds about in the sky and she was grateful for any cool breeze. The clouds had been gathering during the morning and it could turn into a really bad storm by tonight. There was something else, though. Something was going to change, for good. Forever.

"Petunia!" Miranda shouted from the side of the house. Petunia jumped half out of her shoes and dropped all the herbs she had been picking. Miranda forgot that any raised voice at a slave was probably one used in anger, and the poor house slave thought she was next for the whipping post.

"Petunia," Miranda said again in a much softer tone. She stepped into the garden near the rosemary and Andy stayed on the border. "The herb you used for Father's tea this morning, what is it called?"

Petunia was so startled at the earlier cry that she stared at Miranda for a moment, dumbfounded. She looked at the ground, then at the sky, her eyes moving back and forth, her lips moving as if she were talking to herself.

Fear can make a person, even one as knowledgeable as Petunia, lose her memory.

"The master's tea, was called..." Petunia searched her brain. The more she searched, the less she found. The more time went by, Miranda got more impatient.

"Good night, Petunia! It was just this morning!" Miranda scolded.

"I'm sorry, Miss Miriam, I'm trying to think!" Petunia said.

Andy touched Miranda's hand. "Keep it cool, girl," the touch said.

Petunia looked around the garden at the myriad of herbs. Nothing looked right.

Jasmine?

Cucumber?

Rosehips?

"No, that's not right," she muttered. "The tea was for the cough, which was for the lungs, which cleaned out the fluid in the lungs which..."

"Sassafras!" she said with a sigh of relief.

"*Sassafras*!" exclaimed Andy and Miranda at the same time.

"Where can we get some?" Miranda asked.

"I used the last of it this morning for the tea!" the frightened Petunia wailed. "I collected it late last summer, dried it, and used most of it during the winter and spring. There was a little left when Miss Nancy asked me to make a pot for the master."

"And now there's *none* left?" asked Andy in disbelief. "Not one teeny, itsy bitsy leaf of it left?"

Petunia didn't know what "itsy bitsy" meant, but she could figure it out.

"No sir," she said. Her legs were starting to shake under her dress, and she thought she was a goner.

Andy mentally slapped himself. *Intimidation is not the answer.*

"Petunia," he reassured her, "you're not in any trouble. We're not angry with you. We just wanted to know what the herb was called. Where did you go to pick the sassafras?"

"Do you know just beyond the slave quarters, on the other side, by the road, there is a row of trees and hedges that separates the quarters from the fields?"

"Yee-s," said Miranda tentatively. "I can find it."

"The sassafras trees are in there, in among the other

trees. I plan on picking a new harvest starting this weekend if you want to go with me. I can show you then."

"What do they look like?" inquired Andy.

Petunia's voice had regained its confidence.

"First of all, you notice the smell. But mostly, they have reddish leaves, and the trees can grow very tall - up to a hundred feet. But it's easy to reach the leaves and pick them. Twigs too. Look for the trees with the berries. That's the sassafras."

Miranda and Andy relaxed. It was the answer they wanted to hear. *Easy to reach the leaves and pick them.* Andy wanted to kiss Petunia right there on the spot, he was so excited, but all he did was say thank you.

Andy told Miranda he would go over to Roger's cabin and draw the X in the dirt if she wanted to go find the sassafras. All they had to do now was wait until Roger met them that night, light the leaves, and say farewell to the 19th century.

At Roger's cabin, Andy drew the X and right underneath it, he wrote, “going home” in very small letters. He asked Grandma Geri to guide Roger to see these words, and he hoped that Roger was not seriously hurt. "I don't know what else to do," Andy said to her.

"Forgive yourself," Grandma Geri said. "And learn."

Miranda ran over to the hedges and trees that Petunia had described, and easily found the sassafras. It was ripe for harvest this time of year, and the closer Miranda got, the stronger the smell became.

Sassafras.

She found the reddish leaves and felt them. She even smelled them, selfishly hoping it might just send her off. No such luck.

"They have to be burned," she said. "No other way around it. It's the smoke that sends you flying."

She picked eight or nine leaves and crammed them into her dress pocket. She wanted to make sure that when they burned them, there would be enough smoke for everybody. She picked six more leaves just in case.

Nobody was around this time of day, and Miranda sat on a rock and looked at the view. The fields stretched out in front of her, behind her were the last of the slave quarters. She watched as the slaves harvested the crops, and she saw Moxley riding around going from group to group.

She didn't see Roger, but she knew he was out there somewhere. Picking. Hurting. Swearing. Hating. She hoped not the last one. She saw the hatred in Moxley's eyes this morning: his sick looking grin, his face melting into pleasure every time the whip hit Roger, and it frightened her. She stood up to him simply because her fear had made her angry. She'd never seen that depth of hatred in one human being for another.

"What a lousy time to be living in," she said. "Selling and buying people! Owning people. Hating people!"

The Georgia landscape was beautiful. The clouds had cooled the land a little, and the earth was ripe with harvest smells. Pears, plums, berries, cotton, corn, beans, tomatoes. But Miranda didn't care about the smells, the beauty of the land.

*I've never been to Georgia before*, she thought. *I'm sure it's nice, now. But this? This world is ridiculous. This is completely unacceptable. And I refuse to accept it.*

She stood up and thrust both fists in the air.

"Good riddance!" she shouted.

With her crushed leaves, she turned around and walked back to the Main House for supper. She couldn't wait to get rid of this cumbersome dress and run around in shorts again. She couldn't wait for the 21st Century.

In ten hours, the night would fall, and Andy, Miranda, and Roger would meet in the barn, light the leaves and vanish.

None of them knew that Moxley, too, would be up and about that night. Whenever there was a whipping, it was common for the overseer to secretly keep watch during the night looking for signs of revolt.

# Chapter Twenty-Two

No one had spoken to Roger all day in the cornfield. Uncle Steven and Aunt Rose avoided him. They were ashamed of him, and all afternoon Moxley watched them closer than any of the other slaves. Moxley had even gotten off his horse once and slapped Rose for not working fast enough.

Workers nearby talked about Roger behind his back when he was out of earshot.

"Just what we need, some young boy thinking he can out-whip the whipper. Every time there's a whipping, Moxley gets meaner than ever!"

"Something's not right today, no sir, I can feel it, something bad is coming," said one of the intuitive ones.

"I think something bad already happened!" said a companion.

"No, I mean something worse. Look at the clouds, even they are dark. It doesn't smell right, no sir, the time does not smell right." He shook his head and hoped that whatever was coming, wouldn't happen to him.

At 8:30, Rufus and his family marched to their cabin from the fields. "Go out and get the vegetables, Rufus," Aunt Rose said the moment they stepped inside the doorway. She hadn't said a word to him all day, and Roger knew she only said *that* out of habit.

Roger's legs were cramped and his neck was stiff. His anger, having been stifled all day, uncontrollably rose to the surface. He stomped over to the bed and punched it hard. "This is not my life!" he said. His eyes pierced into his aunt's face as he spewed out the words. "When I see that kid again, I swear to God I'm going to rap his mouth so hard it'll make his teeth fall out." Roger punched that bed a second time. "And I don't care who hears me!" He punched it again.

"Go ahead," Aunt Rose said, sitting down on the wooden stool next to the fire. Her voice was as quiet and as tired as the sunset. "You just go ahead, and swear to your God and hit and punch. Why stop there, Rufus? Why stop at hitting him? Why not kill him? Go ahead, tell the whole world how you're going to break out of all this," she pointed to the cabin, the floor, the dirt, "and claim your justice."

Roger looked out the cabin doorway toward an impossible freedom, then back into his aunt's loving eyes. He pulled his knees up to his face and cried. He cried because of the pain in his back and the anger in his chest.

He wiped his nose on his pant leg. "What am I supposed to do? Let him get away with that? Let that little son of a -"

"Rise above it, Rufus. That boy has nothing over you, because you are and forever will be a human being. You are my sister's son. You are your brothers' joy. You are my nephew and my family. What you do affects us all."

The air was quiet for a moment. Roger dimly heard other people in other cabins chopping wood and chopping vegetables.

"I'm sorry, Aunt Rose. I'm sorry I got the family in trouble."

"'Sorry' doesn't put food on the table, Rufus. Go on now, your brothers are hungry."

Roger slid out the door and slinked over to the garden. There, in the dirt, was the X and the "going home" words. He stopped and stared at the words like Andy did when he saw the rattlesnake.

"Going home."

*Going home!*

Roger felt a victory cry traveling up his throat, and he put his hands over his mouth to keep the noise from leaking out. It's over! They must have found the herb! He was leaving! No more bending and picking. No more aching! No more lumpy bed with bugs crawling on him and damp floors and smoky cabins. No more vegetables that gave him diarrhea.

Roger did a slight dance, and looked toward the barn. Finally! He, and Miranda, and Andy would ... .

Andy, he thought. *I hate him. I really do.*

Roger bent down and yanked up a turnip. He tossed the turnip lightly into the air feeling the texture of the vegetable as it came down and landed in his palm. He did it again and again. Squatting like this in the tiny vegetable patch, the earth smells, the barn smells, the *reality* of this world was stronger now than any time spent in the fields.

He was black, Andy was white. He had taken the fall. He had spoken sooner than Andy because he knew that it would save his family. He hadn't wanted Aunt Rose and Uncle Steven and even Pete and Leeks to suffer because of his silence. He took the fall.

He recalled Andy's sad face just before the first lash fell. He was just as tortured as Roger was. It was a lose/lose situation. Andy *had* stopped it, though. He stopped at “ten” versus going on to “fifteen” or even higher.

But why didn't Andy stop at “one”?

Roger grabbed an old, rotten potato and hurled it as hard as he could. He heard it go *SPLAT* when it hit a tree.

What do you do with that?

Roger didn't know. Alone, hungry, his back on fire despite the pork fat Aunt Rose had silently, angrily rubbed into him that morning, Roger knelt in the Georgia red clay dirt. Andy Mackpeace was his best friend. When he couldn't talk about certain things to his folks, he could talk to Andy. When he felt stupid, or inconsequential, hanging out with Andy made him feel comfortable and secure. Their lives, at times, could not be more diverse. Roger was on the baseball team; Andy wasn't. Andy loved to camp out, go fishing, be quiet in nature; Roger could take it or leave it because sometimes all that silence really bored him. Roger could probably create a whole list of differences between them, but something connected them ever since he caught Ronnie Thurman beating Andy up. He knew now that he shouldn't have interfered, just let Andy deal with it himself, but the injustice of that brute infuriated Roger, and he had to step in. To beat up another kid just because you can, because you're bigger, is wrong. It's just plain wrong. Well, that's what he thought, anyway. And ever since then, he and Andy were bonded in a way that transcended time.

And now this. He never thought there would be a time when his best friend would turn the tide and beat him up. Not just beat him up, but whip him! Humiliate him in front of all his people!

Roger got angry all over again. He pounded the dirt with his fist, counting out loud, pounding as if to throw into the earth all his anger, his frustration at this horrible life. He swore, and cried, and pummeled the ground until he grew tired, until his knuckles hurt from the impact.

As the sun started to hit the horizon, a breeze picked up. He looked at the dirt under his fingernails, the dirt in the cracks of his hands, and his anger was replaced with a new sense of pride. *This dirt is my history*, he thought.

He hoped that when they returned to New Hampshire, the dirt would stay in his hands.

Despite the misused power, despite the impossible odds, Roger survived. He hadn't caved in. In the face of such a horrendous situation, he had stood firm and proud and tall. That's something he could live with. Andy can wait.

Suddenly giddy with the anticipation of going home, Roger grabbed the turnip and stood up. With the red sun blazing across the sky and the fields, Roger thrust his hand holding the turnip straight into the air and declared, "God is my witness! I'll never go hungry again!"

"Rufus!" Aunt Rose called from inside, "stop that

hollerin' and give me those vegetables!"

"You go, Scarlett," he said to himself.

*     *     *

The time wore on.

Miranda and Andy picked at their dinner and then sat and counted every minute on the clock. Miranda had the leaves all crushed and ready; Andy was in charge of finding a kerosene lantern with a strong, solid flame. He carried his lamp up to his room and when everyone was going to bed, he kept his burning low near the floor, so no one inside the house or outside would see the small light. Andy watched the clock tick, tick, tick, and roughly one half hour after sunset, Andy opened the door, stepped out into the hallway and crept down the stairs, stopping at times, expecting his father to yell at him. No one did.

Miranda was at the barn when Andy arrived. He had put a blanket over the lantern so it wouldn't be seen, but once inside the barn, he threw away the blanket, and it cast a dim shadow on Miranda's excited face. She smiled and nodded as if to say, “this is it!” like the way he felt during the last minutes of school before summer vacation. But when Roger slipped in a moment later, Andy's mood changed. The three of them awkwardly looked at each other, and Andy felt uncomfortable being next to him.

*I'm his enemy*, Andy thought.

"Hi," Andy said. "I'm glad you saw my note."

Roger made no acknowledgement of Andy. "What's

the herb?" he said.

"Sassafras," said Miranda. "I picked it off these trees this morning; it grows right behind the slave quar -" There was no point in bringing up *that* reality again.

"I'm sorry, Roger, I was a coward. I should have told Moxley where to shove his whip and I didn't," Andy said. "That wasn't me. I mean, it was me, of course it was me, but it wasn't, at the same time. I'm sorry, if I could redo the time, I'd ... " his voice trailed off.

He gave up. "There's nothing I can say to make up for this. It's these times, these times is what made people do what they did. We're just visiting, remember?"

The small light from the lantern reflected on Andy's face and his blue eyes were beginning to water.

"I hated you," Roger said. "All day, when I was out there, I hated you. Above all, I wished I had never smelled that damn incense. But I did." Roger heaved a long and deep sigh. "And this is where we are. And this is how they lived. And the more I hated you, the more I realized I was becoming just like them, like Moxley, like Finlayson. A 19th Century incident in a 21st century mind. So, I let it all go. The whip, the punishment, the pain, it doesn't matter anymore; I let it go because it has no power over me. I forgive you, Andy."

Roger viewed the barn walls, took in the smells of horses and hay. "1858 was not exactly a forgiving time," he said. "But I don't live in 1858, and I never will."

"Come," Miranda took Roger's hand. "We're all friends. Let's go home."

She pulled Roger closer to her, and he put his arm around her waist. She dug into her pockets for the crushed herb, and Andy removed the glass from the lantern so that the flame could touch the sassafras. He moved in closer so that the three of them formed a small huddle ready to receive every ounce of the precious smoke that would ensue. Miranda moved the pile of sassafras toward the fire and even Roger could smell the spicy aroma coming from the leaves. Miranda's hand started to shake and she giggled a little bit at the excitement. Roger too started to laugh which, because his arm was around her waist, caused them both to shake even harder.

"Now c'mon!" Andy said through his own contagious laughter. "We have to concentrate. Stop shaking, you two!"

**"You can stop doing everything."**

Moxley stepped out of the shadows from the other side of the barn. He had a rifle in his arms and it was pointed right at Roger. "Get your hands off her."

Roger immediately dropped his arm.

Moxley approached the three frightened travelers and kept his eyes on Roger. "*James*!" he bellowed loudly enough to wake the dead in the cemetery. "*James*! *Come to the barn*!" He never turned his head, and his eyes flared with a coldness that Andy felt in the base of his spine.

"You," Moxley said, gesturing with the rifle to Rufus, "stand over there." He pointed to the wall near the barn door, away from Andy and Miranda.

"Moxley, what are you doing?" commanded Andy.

He tried to use his best plantation owner's son voice, but instead, it came out weak and quivering. "Go to bed, there is nothing for you to do here."

James, at that point, poked his head carefully into the barn door. "Yes, Mr. Moxley?"

"Wake up Mr. Finlayson and ask him to come to the barn. I just found one of his slaves touching and kissing his daughter."

James' face fell open and he was gone.

"No one was kissing, Moxley!" Miranda screamed. They were this close to going home. "You're a stupid, prejudiced woodchuck and I'm sick and tired of your brain-dead point of view on how the world operates! Rufus was protecting me from ... what difference does it make! You get out of here and leave us alone, and that's an order!"

Moxley grinned. He grinned and then laughed. "You don't know nothin' on how this plantation operates, Miss Miriam."

He moved over to Rufus, and while still keeping the gun pointed in his direction, put on a pair of leather work gloves. He took his hand, wrapped it around Roger's throat, and pinned him against the wall of the barn. He didn't squeeze it, he just glared into Roger's eyes. His breath smelled of garlic and he clamped his hand so that Roger couldn't move.

"Don't you even think about running. You ain't going nowhere."

When Moxley had pushed him against the barn wall, Roger felt a piece of wood hit the back of his left knee. The wood was about three feet long, it was used to prop open the barn door on windy days. Roger didn't have to squat down. His left hand naturally brushed against it and he gripped it in his fist. Keeping his eyes locked into Moxley's, it was now or never. Roger shot the woodblock high in the air and aimed it for Moxley's head as hard as he could.

Moxley had thirteen years of being an overseer, and this was not about to be his final year. He saw the quick flash of the wood in the candle's light and his right hand, quick as a snake, left Roger's throat and intercepted the blow.

"You're a dead man," he whispered.

# Chapter Twenty-Three

Fifteen minutes later, the slave quarters' yard was ablaze with light. Near the back walls of the cabins all the slaves stood in a semicircle and waited, and watched. They held lanterns and torches, and the house slaves were standing with them.

Moxley led Roger to an oak tree that grew near the road at the end of the quarters. Roger's hands were tied behind him, and a blindfold was put over his eyes. Moxley, still wearing the leather gloves, "so I don't have to touch your greasy hide," pulled him into the middle of the yard. Aunt Rose and Uncle Steven stood there too, off in the back.

Mr. Finlayson had been awakened, as well as Miss Nancy, and judgment had been finalized. Without another word, the plantation owner stood on the bridge that crossed the little creek and watched the proceedings.

"Drew, Miriam," their father said. "Stand here with me and watch. And learn! This is what happens to slaves who rebel." Andy and Miranda had no choice. No words of protest had helped. Miranda had begged her father to abolish the sentence to no avail. Andy made up lies about meeting Rufus in the barn in order to teach him how to read, but no one listened.

Roger was going to be hanged.

Moxley carried with him a long, strong looking rope. It had only one function: to kill people. A hangman's noose had already been tied. In fact, the knot never came undone. It hung in the barn as a reminder to anyone who walked in there. It was the same rope used to hang the uncooperative wife and her husband. It would now hang Roger.

Moxley threw one end of the rope over the thick branch stretching midway up the tree. He grabbed the end as it fell earthward and he pulled on it several times to make sure the rope was still strong enough to hang a boy. A boy. A fourteen year old boy who, after days of eating very little and working very much, probably weighed one hundred and ten pounds.

"Father, this must stop!" Miranda protested. "This is uncivilized! We study books and learn culture and art and music! We don't *kill* people. We don't *kill* boys!"

"Quiet, girl," Miss Nancy said.

"I will *not* be quiet! You people are animals! You sit in your fancy dining room and eat fine foods and think of yourselves as sophisticated, but this, this! is unforgiveable! This is barbaric! This," as she pointed to Roger as Moxley placed the noose around his neck, *"is insane!"*

Miranda started toward the slave quarters, but her father grabbed her arm with such force that Miranda could not even begin to struggle.

"*You stay here*!" he hissed. "*They* are the animals. Remember that! You are here to lord over swine, not to eat with swine."

Andy watched. He too couldn't move, for in his anger, Mr. Finlayson had grabbed his left arm and didn't let go.

Moxley tightened the noose around Roger's neck. Roger felt this coarse, scratchy *thing* press up against his Adam's apple and for a moment he couldn't breathe. But the noose loosened itself slightly and fell farther down toward his shoulders. Moxley readjusted the rope, moved Roger directly under the tree, and with a grunt and a giant thrust, pulled him up off the ground.

Miranda screamed as if a knife had been plunged into her heart.

Mr. Finlayson, jolted by the noise, instinctively released her arm. The girl's brain suddenly went into hyper drive. Call it genius, call it years of field hockey training, call it the intervention of Grandma Geri, call it whatever you want, but Miranda had a plan. In a dress that weighed at least fifteen pounds, she bolted for the slave quarters. In two leaps she was off the bridge and racing toward the hanging tree. She never heard her father run after her. She stooped down for just a second, like she had swooped up a ball in a hockey game, and grabbed a lantern that was positioned nearby. She heard someone behind her. She heard the breathing, but she never slowed down to see who it was. Through the slave quarters she ran, jumping over pieces of wood and trampling through gardens. She saw the crowd ahead of her, and for a moment she glimpsed Roger's body starting to rise higher and higher. She heard choking noises.

When Miranda screamed, Andy too was released by his father's reaction. He didn't know where Miranda was going, but he knew only one thing: to stop

Moxley. He ran across the bridge toward the crowd of slaves. He butted through them like a crazed goat and headed right for Moxley who was pulling on the rope, hoisting Roger higher. Andy slammed his head into Moxley's stomach, grabbed the overseer's arm and yanked and punched it as hard as he could.

"*Stop*!" Andy roared with all the energy of a bull. "*Put him down*!"

Andy punched Moxley over and over, on his head, his back, his arms, desperately trying to bring the rope down in the opposite direction. He wasn't afraid of Moxley anymore. Andy pulled and panted and wrestled with this dark, foreboding monster.

"Put him *down*!" he yelled again.

Moxley held on to the hanging rope, but took his free hand and punched Andy across the side of his head. Again and again he smacked the boy as Andy's head slammed to the right and to the left. Andy wouldn't let go, but he wasn't winning. Moxley, with the entire weight of his body, shoved him into the dirt and the dust. He kicked Andy in the stomach, and Andy rolled over, the wind knocked out of him.

The stunned crowd was bigger than Miranda expected, and it took her longer to run *around* them. She ran even faster. She saw, by the glow of the lanterns, the shadows and shapes of the sassafras trees growing just ahead of her. There they were: ripe, oozing smells, berries breaking forth with juices. They were clumped and growing on top of each other. Just as she reached the grove, she hurled the lantern with all her might into the thicket, as her father tackled her and pinned her to the ground.

The lantern exploded. The flames shot up and several trees instantly caught on fire. The lack of rain made everything drier and so grasses, bushes, leaves, twigs, started to crackle and produce smoke.

*Burn!* thought Miranda. *Burn!!*

It did burn. The smoke swirled up and around and the wind blew it in the direction of the lynching. A spicy, earthy, yet sweet smell accompanied the smoke, and Miranda coughed and gagged as the smoke poured over her. She breathed in as deeply as she could, and as the trees and the night sky started to disappear and as she felt her father's arms melting into nothingness, the last thought she had was, *Please, let Roger live!*

The smoke swirled around the slaves, around Moxley, around Andy.

"Fire!" someone yelled, and all heads turned toward the source. Moxley barked orders at some of the slaves to put it out, all the while not letting go of that deadly rope.

Roger started to die. He couldn't see anything, so he never saw Miranda start the fire. He didn't know why suddenly he heard lots of screams and yells. The tightness in his neck was unbearable. His body's natural instinct to live kicked in and it fought for breath every single second. He gasped and tried to twist his head around to escape that awful clamping. It made it worse. Roger was lightheaded and soon he would die. The heart would simply stop.

Roger surrendered to the sensation. His final breath was a charred smoke so strong it made his eyes water.

It smelled spicy and earthy and sweet all at the same time. It filled his nostrils and plunged into the last depths of his lungs. Like in a dream, he saw Andy's Grandma Geri talking to him, smiling and welcoming him.

Roger passed out.

# Chapter Twenty-Four

Andy Mackpeace lay on a hardwood floor and heard a bird chirping through an opened window. He didn't move. His eyes were closed. The sun was shining, he felt its heat on his shoulders and back. He smelled freshly mowed grass; it was summer. It was his bedroom. He knew that without proof. When he opened his eyes he was looking directly under his bed. His own 21st Century bed. He saw a pair of his sneakers and a dirty T-shirt that had been thrown under there. This was too good to be true and he thought that if he moved, even one inch, the illusion would snap. Without tilting his head, he looked down at his body, and he was wearing the same shirt and shorts as when Miranda walked into the room, days and days ago. The house was quiet; no one was knocking on the bedroom door. No one was talking on a phone or busy making supper.

Through the bed, on the other side, he saw a body. Miranda. She was lying on her side, and her eyes were open. She was listening, like he was, and adjusting to the sounds of being home. The curtains were blowing slightly and someone was walking outside on the sidewalk. The afternoon was quiet. The steps grew closer to the house, louder, louder, and then became softer as the person walked by.

They lay there together, not speaking, for several minutes.

A small moan came from the foot of the bed followed by a large sob. Andy threw down his silly apprehensions, sat up and crawled over to the noise.

Roger!

Roger was also crunched up on the floor, but he was crying. The impact of what had happened to him crossed between time and space. Andy never saw Roger cry before and Roger had turned over on his side and had his head buried in his right arm, his release of tears getting louder. Andy saddled over to his friend and put his arms around him. Miranda too, had reached the end of the bed. She was at Roger's feet.

"This is serious," Andy said. "I think he's in some kind of shock."

Miranda put a hand around each of Roger's ankles and held them there willing him to come back to himself. He was trembling under her, his legs were shaking. Miranda gracefully took off Roger's shoes and started to massage his feet. With tenderness and care, she placed the palms of her hands against his soles and didn't move. She held herself very still. This was what she knew to bring him back.

Andy spoke to Roger in a whispered voice, so soft that Miranda wouldn't hear him. He leaned close to Roger's ear and repeated some words over and over.

Comforted by Andy's voice and Miranda's healing massage, Roger miraculously calmed down. He rolled onto his back and his tears streaked down the side of his face. Andy could see he was embarrassed at being seen like this.

"Stupid, huh," Roger said. He lay there, breathing

heavy, adjusting to the sensation of Andy's floor beneath his back, the bright white ceiling above him, the smells of New Hampshire creeping back into his reality.

"Not to me, Rog."

He stopped crying and looked up at Andy. "We're home, right? I mean, home, home?" he asked, wiping his nose on his T-shirt.

"Yes," Andy said, "we're back. And you're alive." He touched Roger's neck. "Are you in any pain?"

Roger shifted his arm and felt his neck. "Nothing. It's as if it never happened. There's no mark on me or anything, right?"

"Not a thing," smiled Miranda. "Not a blooming thing!" She laughed at the absurdity of it all. That world was gone. They were safe. They were home. They had escaped unscathed and they knew it.

Andy looked for the dropped incense stick. It was in the same place as before, along with the matches and the compass. Time had not passed at all.

"It's still Wednesday," he said. "Nothing's changed. No one is even home yet." He got up and collected the spilled items. He placed the incense stick back into the little box but in a separate drawer from the other sticks.

"What are you going to do with those?" asked Miranda.

"I don't know yet," said Andy. "I know it's stupid to hang on to them, but I don't think Grandma Geri would want me to throw them out. Suppose someone found them and got whisked off without being prepared?"

Roger was sitting up now, smiling, checking his

body for signs of injury. There were none. Andy put the incense box in his closet, on the top shelf. He rejoined his two friends on the floor, and they stayed in that circle for a long, long time.

# Chapter Twenty-Five

Time, eventually, would bring home Andy's mother and then his father, and dinners would be made and cleared up, and vacations planned and taken. Time and summer drifted on, one day after the other in their lazy feelings of freedom and relief. The three travelers took no more incense trips. Andy and Miranda started volunteering at the vet's office on Saturdays and Sundays. Uncle James took Andy on a three-day fishing trip. One night, in late July, Roger sat Andy and Miranda down and told them some unexpected news. His father had been offered a job in Montana and after discussing it with the family, he had accepted. Andy was quiet when he told them; his best friend was moving away.

"We still have the summer together," Roger said. "I don't leave until Sept 1st."

Roger was so busy packing up his home that, despite his good intentions, he didn't have a lot of free time to spend with his friends.

Andy was sure it meant something else. "He hates me," he said one day to Miranda when they were walking to the vet's. "He doesn't want to be my friend anymore, after what happened to him, after what my stupidity caused him. I don't blame him, I dropped the stick. Me, nobody else, me!"

"Give him some time," Miranda advised Andy whenever they talked about it. "We were given a chance to see what life was like back then ... for us, for Roger. I know it's taken me a while to get used to the fact that I traveled back in time, met someone like Petunia, Moxley. It's the same for Roger ... only different," she paused, "only worse."

Andy couldn't let it go. The mistakes of his choices haunted him. The guilt of not being perfect, even in time travel, was eating him alive. Four days later, while walking home from Silver Lake, Andy stopped in mid step.

"It's all my fault, Miranda, I dropped the stick," he stated for the twenty-third time. Miranda had been counting.

She took two quick steps ahead of Andy, whirled around and grabbed his arms. "That does it!" she yelled. "Look at me. Enough with the self pity, because you're driving me nuts! You stood up to Moxley and you fought for Roger's life. I don't think Roger's holding what happened to him *against* you. But if he is," Miranda said shaking Andy with every word, "and if he's ditching a great friend like you, then it's his loss."

Miranda released his arms. "Andy, please, let it go! It's like the rope marks on his neck, remember? There aren't any."

Andy had a dream about Grandma Geri that night. She was laughing and playing some kind of board game with him. Andy woke up and felt his grandmother in the room with him. He didn't turn on a light; he wasn't scared, it simply felt like she was standing there, near his bed.

"Grandma Geri?" he asked. "Are you a ghost?"

"I am *not* a ghost!" she said. "I'm merely checking on you is all. Whenever you think about me or 'feel' me, you can pretty much be sure, I'm thinking about you too."

Andy Mackpeace started to cry. He was sitting up in bed, but he threw a pillow over his face to hide the noise.

"I miss you too, Andy."

Andy lay back down and turned over on his side. He closed his eyes, but Grandma Geri didn't go away. He was glad she didn't.

"I don't have those awful dreams anymore, Grandma. They went away."

"You turned around and faced the demons, didn't you. You told them to stop."

"Moxley wasn't what I had in mind, but it's the same thing, isn't it."

Grandma Geri was silent. Andy sensed that she was there, just listening. Someone else came to his mind.

"Don't make Roger go," he said.

Andy felt Grandma Geri sit down, like a presence, she took up space on the lower left side of his bed.

"I have no control over that one, Andy. You have a special relationship with Roger. Don't you see that?"

"I see that, yeah, I do."

"Then what are you worried about? Oh, Andy, you have so much strength and intelligence and," she laughed and kicked her feet up off the floor. "Wonderfulness! Roger sees those qualities. Don't you see them?"

Grandma Geri continued to swoosh her feet through the air. "You're a pretty neat kid to have on the home team."

On Friday, August 26, Miranda Roberts walked over to Roger's house. She knocked on the door and when Roger opened it, she saw his parents hustling around inside. Open boxes of dishes and glasses lay on the floor. Rolled up rugs and blankets were piled on the stairs. Roger stepped outside and closed the door behind him.

"Hi," he said.

"I'm going to the Jersey Shore tomorrow for a week. When I get back, you'll be gone," she said. "So, I came over to say good-bye." Miranda shook her head, embarrassed, and grinned. "I know, we had the 'Farewell BBQ' and then the 'Farewell Swimming Party,' but this, I guess, is it. Whew! I'm having a hard time adjusting to this reality."

"Packing up a house is a lot of work," replied Roger. "Dishes, books, games..."

He stopped. "Andy didn't come with you?"

"He's waiting till the very end. First his grandmother leaves him and now you. That's a lot for one summer. Plus, he believes you secretly hate him for all the trouble he caused or, thinks he caused."

"Good night! When is that boy going to let that go?"

"Roger, I've told him that, I've told him a million times, but I guess he has to hear it from you."

"I'll tell him." Roger's face was calm, calmer than Miranda had ever seen before.

"Life's just too short to go around hating people," he said. "Look at Moxley ... he's long dead by now, and what did all that hatred get for him? Nothing."

"We're growing up," Miranda said.

What she wanted to add was, "You're really wonderful," but what she said instead was, "I hope you like it out there in Montana."

"Well, we'll see." His face grew serious, and he took her hand. "You saved my life. Thank you."

Miranda smiled. "Let's just say I can think fast on my feet."

"Make sure you think twice before sniffing any more of those crazy sticks," Roger laughed. "And if you do, make sure you email me!"

Miranda opened her arms to Roger and then hugged him hard.

"Good-bye," she whispered.

"Good-bye," he whispered back.

As Miranda walked down the driveway, Roger looked up into the late afternoon sky and saw the first "V" of birds migrating south. Miranda suddenly turned around and waved. Roger, surprised, waved back. After that, Miranda didn't turn around again.

Six days later, wearing a jacket for the first time since spring, Andy accepted what he didn't want to face and walked over to Roger's house. The huge moving truck was packed with their furniture and when he approached the house, Roger was bringing out his last suitcase and his bike. His family wanted to be on the road by noon.

"Fifteen minutes to spare!" Roger said looking at his watch, smiling broadly.

"Hi."

They walked away from the truck and the movers. They stood under an oak tree. Some of its leaves had already changed showing the first red of fall.

"It's been one hell of a summer," Andy said.

"It's a lot heller when you've been picking cotton." Roger lifted an eyebrow. "Is that even a word?" He grinned but Andy's face was solemn.

"After we got back, I thought you were avoiding me because of my stupidity. I'm sorry for everything, Roger, I wish I -"

"Andy, stop. Really. There's nothing to talk about. I don't blame you for anything, so stop beating yourself up." Roger playfully punched Andy's arm and gave him a little push. "Okay? All right? There's nothing to feel bad about."

"Okay." Andy blew out a breath of relief. "Okay."

"You're the good guy, Andy, remember?"

"You're my best friend, Roger," Andy said. "You're the bravest guy I know. It's going to be so weird going to school without you, not seeing you every day." He turned a little red, but he said it anyway. "I'm going to miss you ... " his voice broke and he choked up. His eyes clouded over so he swallowed hard and took a breath. " ... I just hope you don't forget me."

"Forget you?"

"Because that's what happens over time, you know, people forget each other. They lose touch."

The wind blew a small, sad breeze, and a colder smell brought the changes of the earth. Roger watched a leaf roll across the lawn. "Time has nothing over us," he said. "We're linked, you and me." His eyes watered and he turned away for a minute. "Years from now, whether it's college or married, or whatever," Roger leaned in and hugged Andy with all his might, "we'll still be friends."

Roger returned to loading his bike and his suitcase. He got into the car that would follow the moving van to his new home. He sat in the back seat while his father drove and his mother waved farewell. Andy watched the car as it headed down the short driveway. As it was about to turn to the left, Roger rolled down his window one last time.

Andy didn't try to stop the tears.

"Goodbye, Andy," he said.

Andy waved back, watched the car till it went over the hill and then Roger was gone.

The neighborhood was quiet, the trees were still. Andy smelled the last cut lawn of summer.

"Do you believe him?" Grandma Geri asked.

Andy thought for a minute. He thought about Moxley and Petunia and even Samuel Maverick. He thought about the tree, that rope, how he looked Moxley in the eye and faced his worst fear.

"Yeah," he said, "I do." Andy wiped his eyes on his sleeve. "I believe him."

"Me too."

The sun was warm, the time was lovely; Andy took a deep breath and let it out again.

"Let's go home," she said.

ACKNOWLEDGEMENTS

Many thanks are owed to the good folks at the Dekalb Public Library in Decatur, Georgia for their services. Also, thank you to Emmy and AK for their tireless feedback. A magnanimous thank you to Joan.

The original artwork for the cover was by Ken Hornbeck. Dina Shadwell designed the book cover lettering.

The sequel to **In the Nick of Time** is called **The Time of His Life**. It is available with CreateSpace Publications, and the e-versions of both books are on www.smashwords.com.

Made in the USA
Middletown, DE
25 August 2015